HARLEQUIN®
Presents

Welcome to a month of fantastic reading, brought to you by Harlequin Presents! Continuing our magnificent series THE ROYAL HOUSE OF NIROLI is Melanie Milburne with *Surgeon Prince, Ordinary Wife*. With the first heir excluded from the throne of Niroli, missing prince and brilliant surgeon Dr. Alex Hunter is torn between duty and his passion for a woman who can never be his queen.... Don't miss out!

Also for your reading pleasure is the first book of Sandra Marton's new THE BILLIONAIRES' BRIDES trilogy, *The Italian Prince's Pregnant Bride*, where Prince Nicolo Barbieri acquires Aimee Black, who, it seems, is pregnant with Nicolo's baby! Then favorite author Lynne Graham brings you a gorgeous Greek in *The Petrakos Bride*, where Maddie comes face-to-face again with her tycoon idol....

In *His Private Mistress* by Chantelle Shaw, Italian racing driver Rafael is determined to make Eden his mistress once more...while in *One-Night Baby* by Susan Stephens, another Italian knows nothing of the secret Kate is hiding from their one night together. If a sheikh is what gets your heart thumping, Annie West brings you *For the Sheikh's Pleasure*, where Sheikh Arik is determined to get Rosalie to open up to receive the loving that only *he* can give her! In *The Brazilian's Blackmail Bargain* by Abby Green, Caleb makes Maggie an offer she just can't refuse. And finally Lindsay Armstrong's *The Rich Man's Virgin* tells the story of a fiercely independent woman who finds she's pregnant by a powerful millionaire. Look out for more brilliant books next month!

Bedded by... *Blackmail*

Forced to bed...then to wed?

He's got her firmly in his sights and she's got only one chance of survival—surrender to his blackmail...and him...in his bed!

Bedded by...Blackmail

The *big* miniseries from Harlequin Presents®.

Dare you read it?

Abby Green

THE BRAZILIAN'S BLACKMAIL BARGAIN

Bedded by...

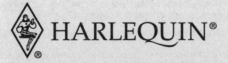

Blackmail
Forced to bed...then to wed?

HARLEQUIN®

TORONTO • NEW YORK • LONDON
AMSTERDAM • PARIS • SYDNEY • HAMBURG
STOCKHOLM • ATHENS • TOKYO • MILAN • MADRID
PRAGUE • WARSAW • BUDAPEST • AUCKLAND

ISBN-13: 978-0-373-12657-6
ISBN-10:   0-373-12657-3

THE BRAZILIAN'S BLACKMAIL BARGAIN

First North American Publication 2007.

Copyright © 2007 by Abby Green.

All about the author...
Abby Green

ABBY GREEN deferred doing a social anthropology degree to work freelance as an assistant director in the film and TV industry—which is a social study in itself! Since then it's been early starts, long hours and mucky fields, ugly car parks and wet-weather gear—especially working in Ireland.

She has no bona fide qualifications, but after years of dealing with recalcitrant actors she could probably help negotiate a peace agreement between two warring countries. She discovered a guide to writing romance one day, and decided to capitalize on her longtime love for Harlequin romances and attempt to follow in the footsteps of such authors as Kate Walker and Penny Jordan. She's enjoying the excuse to be paid to sit inside, away from the elements. She lives in Dublin and hopes that you will enjoy her stories.

You can e-mail her at abbygreen3@yahoo.co.uk.

For Susie Q and again Lynn
my patron saints.

PROLOGUE

London, November

MAGGIE HOLLAND stood just on the other side of the revolving door, the late November darkness throwing the glittering lights of the exclusive London hotel into sharp relief. Her heart was in her mouth, legs shaking, hands clammy and a trickle of sweat ran down her back. Her head ached where pins held the thick mass of curls on top of her head and, with a visibly trembling hand, she pulled the too short mac more tightly around her body. The cold wind whistled around her exposed legs but couldn't shock her out of the stupor that seemed to have taken control of her body.

A couple clambered out of a cab on the street just behind her and, in a flurry of doormen, luggage and broken German on the cuttingly cold breeze, she knew she had to move into the lobby just behind the glass or move aside and let them pass.

The stupor passed; reality rushed in. Taking a deep breath, she didn't move aside, much as she wanted to, but pushed the revolving door and stepped into the warm foyer.

She saw him as soon as she walked in. Impossible to miss him; he would draw the eye of anyone with a pulse.

He was standing facing away from her, talking to someone,

so hadn't noted her arrival and she was glad of the respite. A chance, however flimsy, to gather herself and her exposed nerves. And a chance to observe him for a moment.

He stood with hands in his pockets, making the material of his tailored trousers run taut over his behind, drawing attention to a powerful physique that was more like that of an athlete in his prime than a corporate tycoon worth millions… some even said billions. A tycoon who had a fearsome reputation as one of the most innovative and powerful in Europe.

Caleb Cameron hadn't existed in her world until two weeks ago, when she'd met him at her stepfather's house for the first time. Never an enthusiastic visitor unless requested by her mother, that had been one of those times when Maggie's mother had begged her for some support. He had been one of a few assorted businessmen who in the last two weeks had conducted intense meetings with her stepfather. And having been there nearly every day to help her mother hostess, Maggie's every waking and sleeping thought had quickly become filled with this dynamic man, and still the disbelief that he could possibly be interested in *her*. Proof of which was this date tonight.

Her mouth compressed. A date which had been hijacked for other ends.

Maggie swallowed with difficulty. She couldn't escape what she had to do. She knew that with an awful fatality. But…surely he would see through her in a second? She almost hoped he would. He had a rapier-sharp intellect. And yet *she* was somehow expected to…no, had been *ordered* to be the one to… Her mind shut down; she felt sick again and shut her eyes briefly.

All she wanted to do was turn around and walk back out of the door. But she couldn't. If she didn't go through with this, the consequences didn't bear thinking about and affected the one person dearest to her. She had no choice.

'Maggie.'

Her eyes snapped open. How had she not heard him approach? An impression struck her of a large, lethal, graceful jungle cat. She strove for calm, straightening her spine.

'Caleb, I'm sorry. I hope you weren't waiting for too long.'

He skimmed a look up and down, leaving her a little breathless, a broad shoulder lifted negligently. 'A few minutes is a pleasant surprise. I've been kept waiting for longer.'

Somehow Maggie knew *that* was a lie. No woman would keep this man waiting. His penetrating blue gaze held hers captive. She couldn't look away and that familiar boneless feeling permeated her, making her blood slow and throb through her veins. This was the effect he had had on her ever since she'd laid eyes on him. When she'd been innocent of the part she was being primed to play in her stepfather's Machiavellian plans. When she'd been aware of nothing more than Caleb…as a man…not someone who had to be betrayed, ruined…plundered for his wealth.

And now…seduced.

Looking up at him, her mind was scrambled. For a second she could almost fool herself into thinking that what was outside didn't exist. Maybe this really could just be the simple date he'd asked her on…with no agenda. That thought made her breathless with a dangerous excitement. She wasn't aware of the slight ironic smile that touched her lips at her wishful thinking. After tonight she'd never see him again and that made her insides feel hollow.

An icy gleam lit Caleb's eyes for a split second, but then it was gone, replaced with benign politeness. 'Shall we? The dinner table is ready…'

Maggie's heart plummeted. *This was it…no turning back.* 'Fine.'

On wooden legs she preceded him through the foyer to the doors at the other end. She felt as though she was walking to the guillotine. And then, to compound it, the heavy room key in her pocket brushed against her leg. Nausea clawed her stomach again. The key to the room upstairs that had been booked by her stepfather. The scene where the seduction was to take place. He even had his man there somewhere, in the shadows, watching, monitoring proceedings…to make sure one or the other didn't leave too soon. Before the damage could be done.

Dear God. How could she do this?

At the door to the dining room she felt Caleb's fingers on her shoulders. She half turned, acutely aware of the bare scrap of lace she was wearing. The excuse for a dress that *he* had bought for her to wear. She wanted to halt the inevitable slide of the coat from her shoulders even as the *maître d'* came forward to take it. Panic rose. She couldn't do this…she couldn't look. Couldn't bear to see the reaction on Caleb's face when he saw her outfit.

She was wearing a slip. That was all. He'd seen more clothes on a lap dancer. It didn't suit her pale colouring. The rich red hair was pinned up, making his fingers itch to take it down. A curious burning disappointment licked through his veins as he realised that, even in the cheapest outfit, she still had the power to ignite forceful desire in his body. The tingling awareness of which was making itself very apparent. And something else licked through him too. Self-derision. For a brief moment, before he had found out who she was, or what was going on, he had thought… He tried to stop his thoughts going in that direction. But his mind refused to obey.

When he had first met her, something deep and hidden and *unknown* had been touched. He had been shaken out of his usual cynical inertia. She had looked at him that first time with such sweet shyness and had then smiled. That smile had captured self-deprecation at her response, the current of sexual awareness running between them and something so intangible…but so innocently feminine, that he'd felt a lurch of surprise. He was used to women smiling at him, but usually with such blatant calculation that his blood ran cold.

His mouth thinned as he followed her through the dining room; he was aware of the openly admiring glances she was getting, the sexy sway of her hips, and his eyes, like theirs, were drawn to the scrap of lace and silk that was barely decent. To see her tonight, with her intentions so disappointingly *obvious*, he wondered again how he could ever have thought he'd been surprised…or that she wasn't exactly the same as every other woman.

He knew with confident arrogance that she wanted him. She had felt the same immediate impact on first sight—he knew *that*. But she probably turned it on for everyone, no distinction being made.

She was nothing more than a mediocre actress, but yet…and he hated the admission, she'd almost fooled him, got under his guard. He'd never had a lapse in his attention before now, keeping corporations going in every major city from Tokyo to London. He knew the minutiae of every single one of them, his control legendary and fear-inducing among his competition. A skill that would not let *her* or her family undermine that control, even now, when they thought they had him. The fools.

He focused on the facts.

She was here to take him to bed, to seduce him and distract him. To act as the honey trap. One of the oldest tricks in the book. If he wasn't mistaken, he was sure he'd seen the distinctive shape of a key in her pocket as he'd taken her coat. Was it a key to a hotel room there? The disgust rose like bile.

But two could play at that game; he was here to seduce her too. A little luxury he was affording himself, the spoils of war. Because this was war. Since he'd felt that punch to his gut on first sight, had then discovered what their little game was, the way she'd so blatantly been put on display for him…he'd been determined to sample what was on offer.

They reached the table.

Maggie walked to the other side and faced him with a look of almost, for a fleeting moment…*unbelievable* trepidation on her face. He mentally shook his head. Hell, she was good. He'd never seen anything like the level of her guile. He reasserted his cool mental clarity, ignored the ache in his loins. The slow burning fire that *would* be sated.

She would soon know just how dismally their machinations had failed. Then he would take his revenge on her family. And then he would be free of this all-consuming desire that held him in its grip.

By the end of the night she would never…*ever* forget him or want to cross his path again.

CHAPTER ONE

Dublin, six months later...

'WE JUST have to meet with Mr Murphy and then it's all over.' In the back of the car as they left the graveyard, Maggie took her mother's hand in hers, concerned by her ashen pallor.

Her mother drew in a shaky breath. 'Love, I don't think I can sit through it...I really don't—'

Maggie tightened her hand in comfort as her mother's eyes filled and her mouth trembled.

She turned stricken eyes to her daughter. 'I'm not sad... Is that terrible? I'm so relieved that he's finally gone; when I think of what I put you through all these years, how I could have—'

'Shh, Mum. Don't think about it now. It's over. He'll never harm either of us again. We're free.'

Her heart ached at the desolation in her mother's eyes, the lines on her face, the lifeless hair scraped back. She had once been a beautiful, vibrant woman. The reason why Tom Holland had wanted her for himself after her father's untimely death. He'd been pathologically jealous of his cousin.

In those days, as a young widow in Ireland with nothing but the house left to her and a small child, Maggie's mother had been vulnerable. When Tom had promised to look after her if she married him, she had thought she was doing the best thing for her and her daughter. It was only after the wedding that his vicious cruelty had become apparent and, in a noto-riously conservative society where divorce hadn't been allowed until relatively recently, her mother had effectively been trapped. Until now.

'Look, you don't have to sit in on the reading of the will; it's going to be a matter of routine anyway. Mr Murphy knows us well enough not to insist on your being there and Tom left everything to you. It's the least he could have done.' Maggie's voice couldn't hide its bitter edge.

'Oh, really love, do you think so? If I could just take a rest…'

'Of course, everything is going to be fine.' Maggie tried to inject upbeat energy into her voice when all she felt was drained beyond belief.

A short time later the car pulled off the main road in the small village outside Dublin and swept through the gates of a large, welcoming country house. Maggie took a deep com-forting breath. The first glimpse of the house through the trees that lined the short drive never failed to lift her spirits. It had been their own family home—her father and mother's. It was the one thing her stepfather hadn't got his hands on. A link back to happier days, the memories of which she knew had helped her mother get through the worst times. It was here she and her mother had moved back to six months ago, after that… Even now she couldn't bring herself to think of that night. The pain in her heart was still acute, despite her attempts to ignore it, deny it. The awful humiliation was still vivid.

Luckily her mother had listened to her and they'd left London almost immediately. By the time Tom had realised that his plan hadn't worked he'd been too caught up with his business to come after them. And now he was gone for good.

Dead. She brought her mother up to her bedroom and was almost at the door when she called her back.

'What is it, Mum?' Maggie walked over and sat down.

Her mother's eyes were suddenly bright and serious. 'Promise me you'll never speak of what happened to us… what Tom did to us…I couldn't bear the shame.'

She was used to this recurring plea of her mother's. 'Of course not…you know I never have; why would I now?'

Her mother grabbed her hand with surprising strength. 'Promise me, Margaret.'

'I promise.' She pressed a kiss to her mother's forehead and left again. It was a promise she wouldn't find hard to keep; she had no intention of talking or thinking about Tom Holland ever again if she could help it. Maggie went back downstairs and heard the sound of a car. The solicitor. After hanging up her coat, she quickly smoothed back her hair, opening the door with a smile as the bell sounded. She had always liked the small man with twinkling eyes. Unlike the rest of Tom Holland's coterie of hangers-on and staff, his local Dublin solicitor had also been her father's solicitor.

She showed the older gentleman into the front room. 'I hope you'll excuse my mother; she's not feeling the best.'

He turned to face Maggie, 'Nothing serious, I hope?'

'No,' she quickly assured him, knowing of his genuine concern. 'She's just tired and drained from the past few days. But if you need her here—'

He put up a hand. 'Actually, maybe it's better if she doesn't hear what I have to say.' Suddenly he couldn't meet Maggie's eyes and shifted uncomfortably on his feet. A sliver of fear made her stop breathing for a second. It was too good to be true that Tom Holland was gone. She knew it.

'What do you mean?'

'Maggie let's sit down. I'm afraid I've got some bad news.'

She moved numbly to a chair and watched as the solicitor sat down near a table and put down his briefcase. He didn't take out any papers. She struggled to stay calm, despite his bleak face.

'What…what is it?'

He looked up at her finally, his hands stretching out, palms up, empty. 'I'm afraid that you and your mother have been left with nothing.'

Her heart started to beat normally again, as she relaxed. It wasn't too bad. She and her mother hadn't ever received much from Tom and she had been supporting herself for years since college and was building a modest income from her paintings.

'Well, that's not the end of the world, is it? But…but where did it all go?'

They were talking about millions of pounds after all. Mr Murphy sighed; he hated being the bearer of bad news. 'It would appear that one of his adversaries finally brought him down, lock stock and barrel—the timing is most unfortunate. A tycoon in the UK that your stepfather attempted to take over some time ago has been steadily buying up stock, taking over his companies and on the day Tom had the heart attack the last of his businesses crumbled—a freak coincidence.'

That would explain his absence, why he hadn't followed them home, demanded her mother return to London, *punished them*. Despite the dire news, Maggie couldn't help the spike of satisfaction that rushed through her; she only wished she could have seen his reaction when he had found out.

'Well, there's nothing to be done now; at least we have our house.'

The words fell into the space between them and Maggie watched with growing dread as she saw Mr Murphy's eyes flicker away guiltily and his hand went to his collar as if he needed air.

'Mr Murphy, we do have this house, don't we? It's my mother's.'

He shook his head slowly, as if he couldn't even bring himself to articulate the words. At Maggie's desperate look he had to. He cleared his throat and it sounded harsh in the silence of the room.

'My dear…nearly a year ago in London your stepfather persuaded your mother to sign over this house in his name as collateral. God knows how he persuaded her; maybe she didn't understand what she was doing…I'm afraid it was tied up with all of his other assets. It now belongs to—'

Just then the sound of a car outside the window stopped his words. Maggie couldn't move; she was in shock. She couldn't even begin to figure how her mother had done such a thing; this house was sacrosanct. Rage and disbelief warred inside her as the information sank in.

Mr Murphy was looking out of the window. 'That's him. The head of the corporation. He came to see me personally and insisted on coming here today to see you and your mother. I'm so sorry, but he refused to be dissuaded.'

When the doorbell rang and Maggie didn't move, Mr Murphy finally got up to answer it. She was numb, barely aware of the sound of the door opening, footsteps approaching, the deep timbre of a voice answering something the solicitor had said. Maggie looked up and suddenly her world stopped turning. She felt herself standing slowly as if moving through treacle, her limbs sluggish and unwieldy.

Caleb Cameron. Larger than life, his huge frame filling the doorway. He cocked his head slightly and a mocking smile touched his lips. His eyes captured Maggie's and she couldn't look away. They were glacial, moving over her, stripping her. The man who had turned her world upside down that night six months ago was back…apparently to turn it upside down again. She fought strenuously against the shocking pull she could feel in every cell as she reacted to his commanding aura. The room seemed to tilt slightly on its axis as she unconsciously sucked in a breath, her need for oxygen necessary but secondary to the shock after shock that she was reeling from.

Unable to tear her eyes away from his in morbid fascination, she didn't notice the solicitor precede Caleb into the room and gesture towards her. 'This is Margaret Holland. Maggie, this is Caleb Cameron, he's the man who has taken over all of your stepfather's holdings…including this—'

Before he could say it, she cut in through bloodless lips, 'I know Mr Cameron; we met in London.'

She sank back down on to the chair behind her because her legs were trembling so much they wouldn't hold her up any more and looked up, stricken, as Caleb advanced into the room and sat in the chair just vacated by Mr Murphy.

Despite the urbane, debonair exterior, his body clothed in an exquisite suit, he still exuded that untamed potent maleness she remembered all too well. The virile essence of the man couldn't be contained or disguised by a mere suit. It had bowled her over the first time she had seen him and was having the same effect now, except this time she had the experience of their explosive night together to make seeing him three thousand times worse. And, even though months had passed in the interim, she could feel a hot tide of colour rise up from her chest as countless familiar disturbing images flooded her head.

Caleb exercised iron-willed self-control as he looked her over dispassionately. But despite that effort he couldn't dismiss the heady rush at seeing her in the flesh again. Her face had paled dramatically on seeing him, almond-shaped green eyes huge in her small oval face, the rich abundant hair pulled back severely. The plain black top and straight black skirt couldn't hide the curves he remembered all too well—curves she had flaunted for him…yet now she looked thinner. Somehow fragile. And a protective instinct took him unawares.

A vivid memory struck him just then of seeing her for the first time, her hair falling in a mass of vibrant red curls down her back, like some vision from a medieval painting. Freckles stood out starkly against the paleness of her smooth skin as he subjected her to an exacting inspection. He noticed with satisfaction that her cheeks flooded with hectic colour. If he hadn't known better six months ago, he could have imagined she wore her heart on her sleeve, at the mercy of every reaction showing on that translucent skin. He could have succumbed to a dangerous fantasy. But he hadn't. Because he had known, almost from the very start, exactly what she was.

Maggie Holland was a mercenary bitch who had tried, with her stepfather, to play him for a fool. Never again.

He could see her throat work as she tried to speak.

'You…you've taken over everything.' Her voice was faint. *She was so transparent…*

It gave him such pleasure to know that he was pulling the rug of wealth from under her deceitful feet. He brought his glance, which had shifted to take in the room, back to her face.

'Yes, Ms Holland.'

The implied insult in his use of her surname was obvious and a part of her shrank back.

'As of now, I own every single business interest of your

stepfather's, including this very house. Naturally I declined to take on board his more dubious holdings; the Inland Revenue here and in the UK are currently investigating those and you might find that you're due to receive some hefty tax bills; they have a surprisingly low regard for offshore accounts that haven't been declared.'

Maggie stood up, galvanized into action by the explicit threat in his voice. For the first time since she had seen him again, she tore her gaze away and looked at Mr Murphy, who was near the door.

'Is this true? Can it be possible?'

The older man just nodded his head miserably. She looked back to Caleb, a wild panic rising up. He was utterly unconcerned, as if watching a fly on its back struggling to right itself.

'But…but *how* is this possible? I mean, how can we not have known?' She feverishly went over everything in her pounding head. Even though they hadn't seen Tom in months…how had they somehow missed noticing the dire straits he was leading them to? And how, for the love of God, was it possible that even now he was reaching out from the grave to ruin them…as if he hadn't done enough already?

Because he tried to ruin this man in front of you, with your help…

She shut out the voice with difficulty. She couldn't dwell on that now.

'Mr Murphy…' she implored, incapable of saying another word. Her eyes said it all. The solicitor took her arm and led her to sit down on a couch. She was glad of his protection from facing Caleb alone. She refused to acknowledge him, just feet away, willing him to be gone with all of his threatening words and devastating presence.

'I'm sorry, Maggie, but it is true. Your mother is potentially in debt to the Revenue if they find that Tom was hiding funds in offshore accounts, as they suspect. I can fight the case for you if it comes up, but…' He shrugged.

It was getting worse and worse. Maggie pressed a hand to her forehead.

Caleb stood up with lithe grace and rearranged his cuffs negligently. Maggie looked at him warily from beneath dark lashes, her heart still hammering painfully. 'Murphy, I'll leave the rest to you. Ms Holland, I have nothing more to say to you. I'll expect you and your mother to be out of this house within two weeks; I trust that will give you time to sort yourselves out.' He smiled cruelly. 'I could have exercised my right to take the house today, but would rather you be gone should I decide to move in.'

'Move in…' Maggie repeated dumbly.

'Yes. I'm doing some business in Dublin for a couple of months and need a bolt-hole from the city. This place would serve nicely…' he flicked a dismissive glance around the room '…after I've had it redecorated, of course.'

Maggie stood up again, every inch of her body quivering in anger and reaction, this intrusion into their private sanctuary too much. 'How dare you come in here and speak to me like this, on the very day of a funeral…have you no decency?'

'Decency?' He laughed mirthlessly. They had both forgotten the presence of the other man. Standing close to him, Maggie's head bent back to look up, her throat exposed. She could feel the pulse beat rapidly at her neck. His eyes roved her face contemptuously, his lips curling in obvious distaste at what he saw. 'You have a nerve to talk about decency…or should I inform our friend here exactly what role you played in your own downfall?'

So this was his revenge. He had gone after her stepfather

with ruthless precision and now it was her turn. She looked at him, aghast at his capacity to take vengeance to the very last degree. In his mind she had been just as complicit as Tom Holland and deserved everything she was getting.

Without a backward glance, he strode from the room. It felt curiously flat and drained of colour after his explosive energy had left. She heard the doors close, the car start up, the gravel spurt from under the wheels as he sped away, taking their lives with him. After he was gone, Mr Murphy stood too. Maggie looked at him blankly, still stunned.

'As you can see, your stepfather bit off a little more than he could chew with Cameron. He's never been known to suffer fools gladly and when your stepfather made a second bid to topple Cameron's empire he unleashed the tiger.'

'The second bid…'

'Well, actually, it was the third or fourth… Your stepfather really had a bee in his bonnet about Cameron, saw him as the ultimate prize to win. I know you and your mother weren't aware of most of Tom's dealings. After he tried to take over the Cameron Corporation by legitimate means and failed, he then went underground…and used other tactics, but still couldn't do it.'

Maggie felt sick. She remembered all too well her unwitting role in those tactics. It had been she who had been used in the effort to divert his attention for a crucial moment in time. Thank God Mr Murphy didn't seem to know too much and, after all, it had been in London, not Dublin.

The solicitor continued with a touch of awe in his voice, oblivious to Maggie's turmoil. 'Cameron systematically went through every one of Tom's interests and with a lot more finesse managed to bring him to his knees, which was unusual really; Cameron isn't known for going after his enemies so arbitrarily and mercilessly—he's usually happy to cripple their defences, render them impotent.' He shook his head. 'Tom must have really pushed his buttons…'

Maggie flushed guiltily. 'Well, he's finished us too, it would seem.'

'Yes.' He sighed heavily. 'I've looked at it every which way and he really does have it all sewn up. About the Revenue— I'm hoping if it comes to it that we can make a case…I can try to prove that your mother, while being named in the will, had no other part in her husband's affairs.'

Maggie turned worried eyes to his. 'But we don't have anything any more, no money… How could we afford…?'

He patted her hand. 'Don't worry about that now. I know how hard it's been for your mother. I won't let that man make her life worse than it's already been if I can help it.'

Maggie felt tears threaten at his kindness. 'Thank you.'

With a few more comforting words he got up to leave and, after Maggie had closed the front door, she sagged against it. How on earth was she going to tell her mother? She knew this news would devastate her. For Maggie, her worst nightmare had just happened—coming face to face with Caleb Cameron again. She went back into the front room and, for the first time in her life, with a shaking hand, poured herself a shot of brandy and swallowed it back in one gulp.

As Caleb came to a halt in traffic, he struck the steering wheel with such force that drivers around him looked over, but the light of sudden interest in one woman's eyes went unnoticed. When the lights went green he pulled away sharply, castigating himself. What had he been thinking? He'd always known he was going to ruin Tom Holland after his regular repeated takeover bids—the last one being the closest call. Far too close. The one that had involved *her*. But the takeover wasn't what occupied his thoughts.

He'd told Maggie Holland he never wanted to see her again six months ago and yet, within hours of landing in the country, he had to come and see for himself…stand over his final piece of revenge. He could have left it in the solicitor's hands. So why had he gone all the way out there? To confirm for himself that she couldn't possibly still hold him in thrall?

But it had backfired spectacularly.

To his utter and complete self-disgust, his body had told him in no uncertain terms that she did indeed have the same intoxicating effect. The minute he'd seen her. And yet now he'd made them all pay. So why didn't he feel satisfied? Why was her image burned on to his retina? And how the hell did he think he was going to survive in Dublin for two months, knowing she was in the same city?

As if to dampen the desire, he thought back to that night, when she had done everything exactly as he had suspected. Even down to having a room booked at the hotel. She'd brought him up there and seduced him. Exactly as he'd known she would.

*But yet she didn't sleep with you…*a small voice reminded him mockingly.

Maybe that was it? He'd never walked away from a woman he desired before and yet he'd walked away from her that night. He still wasn't sure why he'd left, when he knew he could have had her…without force. Her attraction had been undeniable, it was in every breathless gasp, every eye-dilating look she'd given him. But when she'd refused him herself at the last moment…somehow he couldn't… He cursed and halted uncomfortable memories. All he knew now was that the unsatisfied ache he remembered had taken up residence again. The ache that had never really gone away if he was brutally honest with himself.

He would have to take a mistress. And soon. He'd been without a woman for too long and that was just what he needed to redirect his wandering attention. And erase Maggie Holland from his thoughts once and for all.

CHAPTER TWO

THAT evening Maggie prepared a light supper and woke her mother up. When they were sitting in the kitchen afterwards she finally asked the question Maggie had been dreading. 'How did it go with Michael?'

She steeled herself. 'Not great. I'm afraid I have some bad news.'

Her mother's fingers clenched around the mug, her knuckles white. 'What is it?'

Maggie could have wept at the familiar stoic look in her eyes. She drove down the lump. 'Mum...someone took over Tom's business... Just the day after he died it became apparent that he had lost everything. Effectively we're bankrupt. It was...' she quashed the potent image of Caleb from her mind's eye '...someone who he had tried to take over.'

'I always knew a lot of people had grievances against him... There was bound to be someone... So what does it mean?' her mother asked.

'Well...' Maggie desperately fought against saying *the house* just yet '...it means that we don't get anything; it's all gone.'

Her mother gave much the same reaction as Maggie had earlier. 'Well, that's not the worst thing, is it? I mean, what have we ever had?' She smiled a watery smile at her daughter

and looked around the kitchen. 'At least we have the house…
Honestly, love, I don't know what I'd do if we didn't have this;
it's all I have left of your father and now I'll be able to live
here in peace.' Maggie's mother reached across the table and
took her daughter's hand, 'Don't look so worried, pet, everything will work out. I'll get a job…you've got your painting;
we'll be okay.'

She hadn't figured it out yet, Maggie knew with a sick
horror. Somehow, her mother hadn't equated signing over the
house as collateral with Tom losing everything.

'Mum…you don't realise. We've lost *everything*…'

Her mother still looked at her blankly.

'Mr Murphy said you signed the house over to Tom before
we left London…'

'Yes, love, but that was just…he just said it was…that it
was only to…' She stopped talking.

'Oh, dear God, what did I do?'

Maggie held her hand. 'It's gone too. It was included in
the rest of his assets.'

Her mother didn't move for some time and then pulled her
hand away slowly and got up to rinse out her cup. Maggie
followed her, worried about her lack of reaction.

When her mother turned to face her she felt real fear, her
eyes were dead, any sign of life or spark gone.

'Mum…'

'Margaret, I can't…don't make me think about this…I
can't bear it.'

She watched helplessly as the bowed woman walked out
of the kitchen and knew that she was struggling with all of
her might to keep herself together. That night she heard the
muted sobs through her wall and knew that her proud
mother would hate her to witness the awful grief. She

couldn't bear to hear her pain. What could she do? There had to be some way out…some solution.

The next morning, as the weak dawn light filtered through the curtains, Maggie lay with eyes wide open after a sleepless night. A night where demons had invaded every thought. Demons that had a familiar severely handsome face. She knew with a fatal certainty what she had to do. What the only option was.

When she walked into the kitchen a short while later any doubts in her head about her plan fled. Her mother was sitting there listlessly. She looked up briefly with shadowed eyes, her face a grey mask of disappointment and weariness. Maggie went and sat down beside her. 'Mum, look at me.' She waited until her mother brought her head around, slowly, as if it were a heavy weight.

'I'm going to go into town for a while…I have something to do, but I'll be back later or first thing in the morning.'

Hopefully with good news…

She didn't want to say too much in case she got her mother's hopes up, but right then and there Maggie vowed with everything in her heart that she would do whatever it took to get the house back in her mother's name. She cooked a light breakfast and forced her mother to have some, relieved to see a slight bloom return to her cheeks before she left.

Once in her small, battered Mini, she stopped by Michael Murphy's office in the main street to find out where Caleb's offices were. He didn't ask any questions, just said as he handed her the address, 'He's not going to be easy to see; everyone in Dublin is begging an audience…'

'I know, but I'll camp outside his door if I have to,' Maggie replied grimly.

She hit the rush hour traffic on the way into town and the

journey, which might normally take thirty minutes, took three times as long.

Finally she was in the city centre and parked near the building in the financial district where Caleb's offices had been set up. She was dressed smartly in her one and only suit. She wanted to look as businesslike as possible. It was dark blue—a skirt and short jacket with a matching cream silk shirt. She wore sheer stockings and high heels and had tied her unruly hair back in a severe bun. She wanted to feel armoured against Caleb's scathing looks and condemnation. Even if she was shaking like a leaf on the inside.

The spring air was deceptively mild, yet she shivered. At reception they directed her up to the top floor, which Caleb had taken over in its entirety for his sole use. Her stomach churned as she ascended in the lift, the thought of seeing him face to face again more daunting than she had thought possible.

Any illusion of ease in getting to see him was swiftly dashed on her arrival on to the opulently designed floor. A veritable bulldog of a secretary was guarding the main foyer and looked Maggie up and down when she requested to see Caleb.

'Do you have an appointment?'

'Well…not exactly, but when he hears who it is he might have a couple of minutes to spare. I won't take up much of his time.'

'I'll let him know, but he has meetings back to back all day. You might be waiting for some time.'

'That's fine.' She'd wait until midnight if she had to. She made a quick call on her mobile to a friend of her mother's in the village, asking her to look in and make sure she was okay. With that done, she settled in for the wait.

Some eight hours later Maggie had run the gamut of emotions: irritation, boredom, anger, despair, disbelief and now she was just exhausted. Her suit was crumpled, her shoes were off and her hair was unravelling. Any make-up that had been there had long slid off. She hadn't left for anything except a crucial toilet visit in case she missed him. All day long men in suits had come and gone. She'd seen lunch being delivered and then taken away again, prompting her own stomach to rumble. The first secretary had been and gone and had been replaced by another similarly bad-tempered one.

Caleb's door opened again and Maggie resigned herself to seeing yet more faceless suits departing and thought dimly that the man's stamina was unbelievable. She didn't register for a minute that it was Caleb himself walking out, his tall, powerful build unmistakable. When her sluggish brain finally clicked into gear, she jumped up, her body protesting at the sudden movement after sitting for so long. He was striding towards the lift, not looking left or right; he hadn't even seen her as she was partially tucked away behind a plant.

'Caleb…' she cursed her impulse to call him by his first name '…Mr Cameron—wait!'

He had just pressed the button for the lift and turned around slowly, his brows snapping together when he saw her. Maggie forced herself to stand tall, only realising then that she was in stockinged feet, her shoes abandoned somewhere near the chair. She hitched up her chin.

'Mr Cameron, I've been waiting all day to see you. I know you're busy, but I'd appreciate just a few minutes of your time.'

'Ivy told me you were here earlier, but she knew I was tied up all day.'

'I insisted on staying…I hoped you might have a window somewhere…'

'Well, as you can see, I didn't. And now, if you'll excuse

me… Call tomorrow and maybe there will be a free appointment.'

He couldn't leave. Maggie stood, open-mouthed. She'd
been waiting for hours without food or water to see him. The
look on his face said he couldn't have cared less if she'd been
bleeding and begging at his feet. He turned away dismissively.

She looked at his broad back, the doors of the lift opening
silently; she had to stop him. She ran forward and put her
hands in to stop the closing doors, looking up into his forbid-
dingly expressionless face.

'Please, Mr Cameron, I'm begging you to just listen to
what I have to say for five minutes. I've been waiting here
since half ten this morning. I know that's my own fault, but
I have to talk to you.'

He stood back against the wall of the lift, casually looking
Maggie up and down as if he were used to women flinging
themselves in his path. Which he more than likely was, she
thought bitterly. He regarded her for a long moment. She
fought against squirming under his look.

'Very well. Five minutes.'

'Thank you,' Maggie let out on a sigh of relief.

He stepped back out of the lift and, with a flick of his hand,
instructed the gaping secretary to go for the night. Without
looking back to see if Maggie was following, he went into his
office. She found her shoes and scrambled to put them on and
follow him in before he changed his mind.

When she walked in warily he was pouring himself a shot
of some dark liquid and sat down at his desk, one large hand
clamped around the glass. Maggie stood nervously, taking in
the dominantly masculine aura of the room. One low lamp
cast a pool of light. The shadows in the room made him look
even darker than he normally did, which, she remembered,

came from his Brazilian mother. His father was the quintessential Englishman and the two sides—one tempestuous and passionate, the other sophisticated—proved to be a heady combination. As Maggie remembered all too well.

'Well?' he asked softly, with more than a hint of steel in his tone.

She took a deep breath. 'It's about our house.'

'You mean my house.'

She nodded slightly, feeling a surge of anger at his proprietary arrogance. 'That house belonged to my father…my birth father,' she qualified. 'It's always been my mother's, the one thing that Tom didn't own.'

'And…?' he asked in a bored tone, vaguely remembering a plain, nervous woman who had hovered around the edges of the meetings in Holland's house.

Maggie moved closer behind the chair opposite his, her hands curling unconsciously around the top, knuckles white. 'Tom made her sign the house over to him. It's always been in her name. I…I don't know how he managed it; she always vowed she'd never—' Maggie stopped herself. He didn't need to know the gory details. 'By taking the house, the only person you're punishing is my mother, and she's got nothing to do with what happened… She's suffered enough—'

'As the wife of a multi-millionaire?' he sneered, his lip curling in disbelief. 'You must be joking if you expect me to believe that. You just want to salvage something and you've concocted some lame sob story—'

'It's not!' Maggie said fiercely. 'Please. You have to believe me.'

'Believe you?' He stood up and advanced around the desk to her side. She stood rooted to the spot. 'You don't have a truthful bone in your body... Tell me, how many other men have you teased for Tom Holland in the last few months... Ten? Twenty? Or maybe you gave them the delectable fruits of your body that you denied me?'

His crude words shocked her into action, wide green eyes stared up and, without thinking about what she was doing, somehow she had moved closer and her hand lifted up, trembling, but before it could reach its target, her wrist was caught. She *abhorred* violence and yet, here she was, about to strike him.

'Now, now... Sheath your claws, you little cat. I don't think you really want to do that, do you?'

With the shock of the near violence and Caleb's hand like a steel clamp around her wrist, Maggie felt her pulse speeding up to triple time. Her eyes drank him in despite herself, taking in the hard jaw, the dark hair swept back off his forehead. The sensuous lips pulled into a grim line. But it was the eyes she remembered the most. Piercing blue—a blue that she'd fancied herself drowning in once...she shut her eyes at the memories...eyes which sliced through her when she opened her own again.

'You can give up the act.' He dropped her hand as though it was infectious and Maggie stepped back; she had to put space between them. She rubbed her wrist absently where he had gripped it, knowing that she'd have a bruise in the morning. She forced herself to look at him again.

'The simple fact is that if you take the house it will kill my mother. It's all she's ever counted on, all that she has to remind her of my father. She didn't get anything from Tom Holland except—'

Maggie belatedly remembered her mother's desperate plea not to reveal the reality of her marriage.

'Yes? Except what?'

This man would never understand. Too much had happened for her to count on any level of trust.

She steeled herself against his overpowering presence, the condemnation in his cold, implacable gaze. She ignored his prompt. 'I know my word means nothing to you, but please just hear me out. She never had anything to do with any of his business concerns and certainly nothing to do with trying to take you down…'

Caleb's eyes narrowed and Maggie seized on a chink in the armour. 'You can ask anyone who knew him,' she said in a rush, 'Ask Mr Murphy; he knows. This isn't for me; it's for her. I'm asking you to put the house back into her name…for *her* sake.'

He just watched her with those hard eyes, his face shuttered. Then he said slowly, 'And all the time your mother was supposedly blithely unaware, you were in league with your stepfather, doing your seductive routine, conning innocent men…and now what? You have a fit of conscience and want to make it up to her? I don't buy it.'

Maggie couldn't fight his opinion of her; it was so low that it may as well have been in the gutter.

She answered with a brittle smile. 'Yes, you could say that's what it is. I'm trying to mend my ways, starting with my mother.' She felt silly tears smart at the back of her eyes. The truth of what she too had suffered at the hands of that man burned like a brand and that someone like Caleb, especially Caleb, would never believe her.

'If I were to do as you ask, how can I be sure you're being altruistic—and what will make it worth my while?'

'I'll do anything you want…anything! Wash floors…' she said wildly, the brittleness gone, sensing a chance, however flimsy. *'Anything.* Just please give my mother back her house; she doesn't deserve this punishment.'

Caleb lounged back nonchalantly against the desk, arms folded across his broad chest, the material of his shirt straining. Maggie couldn't believe that in the midst of all this she could be so aware of him. His gaze was uncomfortably assessing.

He'd already decided he was going to take a mistress, but why go to the tiresome bother of having to go through the motions just to get someone into his bed? When what…*who* he really wanted was conveniently within his grasp. One thing he knew for certain as she stood in front of him, her whole petite frame quivering so lightly that it was barely perceptible—was that he wanted her. Badly. More than he'd ever wanted a woman in his life. And he always got what he wanted…

'You'd sell your soul to the devil?'

'Yes.' She answered simply, without hesitation. 'If I had to.'

'You'd sell yourself to me?' he asked softly.

It took slow seconds for his words to sink in; she wasn't sure if she had heard him correctly. 'I'm sorry—what…?'

'You heard me.'

'Sell myself like…like some kind of—'

'Mistress. You…' He looked her up and down thoroughly, his eyes resting for long seconds on her breasts, which rose and fell, her distress evident. 'Your body to me in exchange for the house.'

Maggie stepped back, blanching at his stark words, his intent, but Caleb stood and advanced a step for every one that she took back. As if she could have ever hoped that she could appeal to just his mercy. Men like him exacted payment for everything.

'I couldn't do that… How…how could you even suggest such a thing?'

'Because, you see, I can. Believe me, I don't want to want you…but I do. And you owe me…ever since you seduced me up in that hotel room six months ago and then turned on the ice maiden act. Tell me, did it turn you on? Was it part of the plan? Did you feel powerful, knowing that you could bring a man to the brink—'

'Stop! It wasn't… I didn't…' she denied automatically, wanting to halt his words, the tide of burning humiliation that threatened to overwhelm her, as she remembered just how awfully wanton she had been, the shock of her response to him. It had been *that*, along with the crushing burden of guilt, that had stunned her into frozen immobility at the time. Everything else had been forgotten. Even her mother. Even the threat. And it had scared the life out of her.

But it had been too late for her to laugh it off or feign non-chalance and then he had dropped the bombshell…revealing just how much he had known all along. Far more than her. Any nebulous desire she might have had to confide in him had died a death right there. He had set out to seduce her as cold-bloodedly as he'd believed she had done. She shivered. And yet there'd been nothing cold-blooded about their lovemaking.

'You tricked me, Maggie. Can you deny that you met me that night with seduction and betrayal in mind?' he asked, making her focus again on the present conversation. A still-ness came into the air around them.

'No…' she replied faintly. Because that was exactly what she had done. Albeit against her will. But if he knew that… He could never know how much she had wanted it to be for real. Finding out the extent of his own deceit when hers had been unintended had exposed a wound that was still far too raw… He'd annihilate her *and* it would bring up all the emotions she'd buried in London, thinking she'd never see him again. She desperately tried another tack. 'But you hate me… How can you want me?'

'I think that you aren't so naïve as to imagine that love or even friendship needs to be involved in the act of sex. I want you—you want the house. It's a simple equation.'

His words flayed her somewhere inside and her hands were clenched tight into fists by her sides. 'But how? I mean, for how long or when?'

'Until I leave Dublin.'

She backed away again, the house, her mother, forgotten. All she could see was the menacing threat in front of her. The dispassionate way he was talking reached down to somewhere deep inside her and she knew that he had the power to rip away the very fabric of herself if she allowed him to do this. She summoned up some last reserve of strength. 'But that's two months... I can't...I won't sleep with you. I couldn't...' she sought feverishly for something to make him back off '...I don't want you.'

'Liar.'

Before she could emit a sound of protest, with lightning speed his arms reached out and he hauled her against his chest, his head descending so quickly that she didn't have time to twist her own away. A hand snaked around to hold it in place, his mouth covering hers, crushing her lips to his. She could taste blood on the tender inner skin of her mouth. Despite the obvious cruelty of the kiss, Maggie could feel an intense excitement explode in her belly, every cell straining to get closer, acutely aware of his absolute maleness and strength.

Then, with a subtle and expert change in tempo, his lips softened, the hand on the back of her head became caressing. His fingers loosening the already unravelling bun, she felt her hair tumble down her back. Her fists, crushed against his chest, could feel his heart beating, the warm skin under the shirt, and they wanted to stretch out, feel, take in the exquisite breadth of it. She shook with the effort it took not to allow that to happen.

With the long wait and no food all day, she was already light-headed; Caleb's potent sexuality effortlessly swept away any resistance. Her eyes closed, Maggie was soon lost in sensation, unaware of anything but the feel of his mouth on hers, hard yet soft. When his tongue sought entry, her mouth opened on a defeated sigh and his tongue touching hers ignited a fire between her legs.

Being in his arms again, with the intensely sensual memories that had never abated…she didn't stand a chance. His mouth moved away and Maggie sucked in a betraying breath until she felt his lips blaze a hot trail down her neck, down to where the pulse beat erratically against her skin. The hand on her back moved lower and pulled her bottom up and into him where she could feel the hard evidence of his desire. She felt every part of her pulsating with the need for him to take her.

That desire transported her back in time and was as effective as a cold douche. She used all her strength to break free. If he hadn't kept his hands on her shoulders she would have collapsed at his feet. Her eyes were glazed, wide and dark green with unmistakable arousal. Her lips were swollen and moist.

The look on his face was triumphant, derision in his eyes at what he thought of her paltry attempt to stop his lovemaking. 'As I said…you're a liar.' He cupped one hand around her chin, tilting her head up inexorably. 'The honey of the honey trap still tastes surprisingly sweet.'

Maggie breathed out on a shuddering breath. She pulled herself away and tried to disguise the trembling in her legs.

'You should be thankful that I still desire you…or you'd have nothing to bargain with.'

His stark words forced Maggie's stricken mind back to why she was there. How could she have forgotten? She focused on them—anything to take her mind off her awful weakness. 'Are you saying you'll give my mother back her house?'

He inclined his head slowly. 'If you give me what I want.'

'Me.'

'Yes.'

Maggie suddenly thought of something and seized on it. 'But…don't you have a girlfriend?'

'What?' he asked sharply.

She flushed at her quick words and the realisation that it might be obvious she'd scoured the papers for news of him—where it was common knowledge that he was never without a beautiful companion. 'The papers…' Her voice trailed off, her cheeks pink.

'Girlfriend!' He laughed mockingly. 'How quaint. I don't think I've had a girlfriend since I was six and living in Rio de Janeiro with my mother. I don't *do* girlfriends, and no, there's no one at the moment, not that you should care, since you have the morals of an alley cat.'

That's handy, Maggie thought slightly hysterically, not even registering his insulting words—plenty of room for the sacrificial lamb to enter stage left. And he was right—how could she be so naïve? This man moved in rarefied circles where the most beautiful and socially acceptable women would be available. Men like him took mistresses until they grew bored or until they needed to marry. And then it would be to the right person, groomed for the job.

Knowing she sounded strangely calm, and knowing it was shock, she asked, 'How would this work?'

'If I'm going to sign the house back to your mother, then be here at two p.m. tomorrow with your bags packed.'

A numbness seeped into her bones. 'You'd expect me to move in with you?'

'Yes. I'll need an escort, companion…and a *willing* lover.'

The word *lover*, never mind *willing*, made shivers of treacherous anticipation skitter down Maggie's spine. She stood stock-still, her hair and clothes in disarray, legs still trembling slightly, her mouth feeling bruised and sensitised.

How had he done this to her? How had she let him?

He had been as guilty as her stepfather six months ago, as far as she was concerned. Both had used her like a pawn in their game of domination. And yet she couldn't help this awful, craving desire that wiped all logic from her brain. That made her weak to him. She hated herself for it. Self-contempt laced her voice. 'What, then?'

'You'll sign a contract that makes sure you get nothing from the deal. The house goes into your mother's name solely, not even to pass to you as inheritance. One condition will be that she can't sell it…just in case that was what you were planning.'

She felt sick. 'God…what they say about you is true; you've already sized up every way I could possibly use this for my own ends. You have no heart.'

A flash of something crossed his face for a split second; if Maggie had been less biased at that moment she could almost have said it was hurt. But *him*? No way. The man wasn't capable of such a feeling. As if to confirm her opinion, his face was like a mask again—it must have been her imagination.

He ignored her words. 'And this will happen when you've given me what I want.'

'When I've slept with you.'

'For two months or as long as I desire you.'

'What if that's only one night?' she said defiantly.

He stepped closer again and stopped just short of her. His

scent enveloped her. She froze. 'Oh, but it won't be, Maggie. I can tell you that much.'

Turning her back for a moment, she sought some respite from his laser-like gaze. Her hands twisted as her mind raced. Their house was worth millions by now… She hadn't a hope of raising that kind of money, and it wasn't about the money. That house was where her mother should be able to live out her days. In peace at last. For Maggie's whole life she had protected her mother. Sometimes more successfully than others. Ever since the first time she'd tried ineffectually to come between Tom's fists and her mother's body. She'd been just six years old and she still bore the scar of that day.

But Tom was gone. This was her mother's last chance of happiness and if she could make sure it happened, undo the wrong that had been done, then she had to. Somehow…and she couldn't think now, not when he was so close…she would have to do this. She turned around again and faced Caleb unflinchingly, determined not to let him see how she had crumbled inside. She hitched her chin. 'And if I'm not here tomorrow?'

At the look on her face Caleb felt a bizarre lurch somewhere in his chest. For a split second he actually wasn't sure if she would do this…and didn't like how that felt. At all. Not after having decided that he would take her as his mistress. He quashed the doubt and the feeling ruthlessly. She was just playing him, probably already trying to figure out how much she could walk away with, which he vowed would be nothing more than he was prepared to give. He stood to his full intimidating height and glanced at the heavy platinum watch that encircled one brown wrist. 'You would now have one week and six days to move out of that house before I move in.'

She watched as Caleb started to walk away, no hint of the

passionate kiss they'd just shared in evidence anywhere. He wasn't tousled and shaking like her. He was cool and almost…bored. As if he did this sort of thing every day. He turned, closing his top button, straightening his tie.

'It's up to you, Maggie. Be here tomorrow or say goodbye to the house. You can let yourself out.'

And then he walked out the door.

CHAPTER THREE

THE next day at half past one, Maggie sat in her car outside Caleb's offices, feeling hot and cold and clammy all at the same time. Her mind lurched from one dead end to another. Going home last night, she'd almost convinced herself that she could persuade her mother that they could start afresh somewhere, let the house go…anything so she wouldn't have to become Caleb's…chattel.

But when she'd arrived home she'd met the doctor on his way out. Panic had seized her, Caleb forgotten. The doctor had been grim. Things were not good. He'd said that he was afraid for her mother's long-term health…her mental health in particular. That he hadn't seen such acute grief in a long time. Miserably, Maggie knew exactly what was wrong.

The house being taken was just the straw breaking the camel's back. And if anything placed her in a position of no going back, this was it. Even though she'd known deep down she'd never have had the heart to deny her mother this anyway. Not when she could do something about it. Not when she'd been partly responsible, however coerced she'd been at the time. She knew with that thought she wasn't really being fair on herself, but the truth was…she *was* responsible. Tom had sucked her into an awful complicity with him. And, however misplaced, she still felt the guilt.

The absolute point of no return had been that morning when she'd informed her mother that, amazingly, Caleb had been merciful enough to leave her the house. But on the condition that Maggie start work for him immediately in recompense.

Maggie had explained that he'd agreed to sign the house back over once she'd started work and moved into the city to be closer. Her mother had been too stunned and ecstatic to question Maggie too deeply. And the difference in her, in the space of even those few minutes, had been nothing short of miraculous, driving the nail into the coffin of Maggie's hopes for escaping her fate.

And now here she was. About to embark on the longest, most treacherous two months of her life. But in the end, if it bought *her* freedom too…then she would cope. Somehow. And she thought she knew how. Caleb thought she was a conniving, mercenary woman of the world…so that was what she would be. He would never see inside the protective shell she was going to erect around herself. Would never see the part of her that was so vulnerable to him. The part that had stupidly believed six months ago…for a brief moment…that he might actually be interested in her. Her mouth compressed. *Oh, he had been*…just not in the way her silly, foolish heart had believed, or hoped. She looked at her watch. Two o'clock. She took a deep breath and opened the car door.

Lifting a hand to knock on Caleb's office door, having been directed there by the unsmiling Ivy, Maggie jumped when it opened suddenly. Caleb stood on the other side, his shirt unbuttoned, showing a few crisp hairs and the smooth brown column of his throat. His rolled-up sleeves revealed muscular forearms and his hair looked as though he'd just run an impatient hand through it.

'You're late,' he bit out.

Maggie made a herculean effort to appear blasé and looked at her watch. 'Two minutes late, Mr Cameron.'

'I take it you're accepting the offer.'

She nodded jerkily. 'If you'll keep your end of the bargain.'

'Of course.' He ran a heated look up and down her body, then focused on her face; freckles descended all the way down to the cleavage just exposed by the V-necked cardigan she wore. His body tightened. 'Don't be late again.'

'I'll do my best.'

They bristled at each other from either side of the door for a few seconds. A muscle twitched at Caleb's jaw. Maggie could feel a light sweat break out on her brow. He reached out and, taking her arm, pulled her into his office, the bizarre moment gone. Once inside, she pulled free and walked to one corner. Caleb went and propped a hip on the side of his desk.

For a moment Maggie was simply stunned by the view that had been obscured by last night's darkness. Windows on all sides gave a breathtaking vista of the bustling city, all the way to the Dublin mountains in the distance. She would have loved to go and study it but kept the awe from her face and resolutely fixed her gaze on him.

'I think we can progress from Mr Cameron to Caleb from now on…I don't like formality in the bedroom.'

'We're not in the bedroom yet,' she snapped.

He stood and was automatically dangerous. Maggie fought against backing away. How was she going to convince him she was a world-weary socialite if she jumped every time he moved? He strolled indolently towards her, coming to a halt just inches away. He was so close that she could see darker flecks of blue in his eyes. 'Oh…we will be. Soon enough. Now, say my name. I want to hear it.'

What? She frowned up at him, opened her mouth to speak and, for the life of her…just couldn't. For some reason, even though she'd called him by his first name only the day before, right now, she couldn't conceive of saying it out loud. It felt as if it had become loaded with some kind of meaning…an endearment of sorts. She shook her head, confusion in the depths of her eyes, a red tide creeping up her face.

He moved closer, bringing a hand to the back of her neck, caressing, finding the delicate spot just below her hairline. 'Maggie…'

Paralysis gripped her. 'I…can't.'

'Maggie. Say it.'

She felt as though she'd been drugged, her limbs heavy, blood flowing thick and slow through her veins. His head was bending, drawing closer…he was going to kiss her. Weakly, she brought her hands up between them.

'Caleb.' It came out huskily, much like a lover would say it. And, in saying it, she knew why it had been so hard. She'd stepped over the line completely. She was his now. How could such an innocuous moment feel so full of meaning?

He stopped and straightened slowly. 'There…now, that wasn't so hard, was it?'

God. She had only been in his office less than five minutes and already she was being reduced to a gibbering wreck. She had to get a grip. Had to play the part she'd planned. The only way she knew how to protect herself.

She moved briskly away, dislodging his hand, and searched her mind for something, anything, to deflect his intense focus. She seized on the first thing and whirled around, a bright forced smile on her face. 'Clothes!'

'What about them?' Caleb was very watchful, arms crossed. He couldn't figure it; in the space of a split second she'd gone from blushing just saying his name to *clothes*? One thing he knew for certain—he couldn't trust her an inch. She was up to something. And, from what he knew of women, that something always amounted to something financial.

Maggie twirled a lock of hair around one finger, something she normally did out of unconscious habit but this time contrived to look as coquettish as possible. 'Well, I expect you'll want me to look my best…and I've left all those sorts of clothes in London…so unless you like this casual look…' She gestured disdainfully at her chain store outfit. She hated this. It went against every sensibility she had to ask for anything, but she wanted him to think the worst.

Her abrupt volte-face jarred with him but then a world-weariness seeped into his bones. She was just like all the others. No different. But then he'd hardly expected her to be different, had he? And he didn't want her in some other man's cast-offs. The very thought made his fists curl. She was his now. She would dress for his pleasure—no one else's.

'Just tell me where and I'll set up an account—you can go this afternoon. I have to go to Monte Carlo for two days tomorrow—something that's just come up—so you can come too. I presume your passport is in order?'

Maggie blanched, her sham of confidence abruptly shaken, and nodded dumbly, taking in the rapid-fire delivery. Monte Carlo? She really was in another world now…

Caleb had moved back to his desk and was picking up the phone, looking at her expectantly, impatiently. Maggie furiously tried to remember his question and mentioned the double-barrelled name of an exclusive store nearby—somewhere she'd never normally go.

After a quick, brusque conversation it was done. Caleb stood and came around to Maggie, tilting her face to his with long fingers. 'Stay away from the cheap tarty stuff, if you can. I don't want a repeat performance of that dinner, where I had to endure every man in the room tripping over himself to get a look at your…' he flicked a glance down to her chest '…assets.'

She burned with humiliation at his mention of the dress her stepfather had forced her to wear. A memory rushed back. Tom Holland's mottled, angry red face in hers.

'You can wear this or go naked. If you don't…you'll be responsible for what's going to happen to your mother.'

Maggie willed the image away and clenched her jaw against Caleb's hand.

'I'll do my best. But I still have the dress, so I might just surprise you.'

The look on his face was chilling. 'Do that and I'll rip it off and dress you myself. Don't play games with me. You won't win.'

A finger of fear clutched at her throat. She didn't know what had made her want to provoke him just then. Of course she didn't still have the dress; it had been relegated to a bin that awful night. She would have burned it if she could.

Finally he released her. She went on wobbly legs to the door. Just as she was about to leave, he called her name. She turned around reluctantly.

'I can use my own car later, so my driver will pick you up when you're done with shopping and bring you to the apartment. Where's your luggage?'

'It…it's in my car. I'll have to pick it up anyway so I can drive to the apartment.'

He shrugged and gave her the address, which she committed to memory. She knew where it was, an exclusive building nearby in the city centre. Then she fled.

Early that evening Maggie pulled into the only parking space left outside the apartment building. The back of her tiny car was piled high with bags. Despite having had a wicked desire to buy nothing but trashy clothes or exorbitant designer outfits…she just couldn't. She was hardwired a certain way and had ended up getting exactly what she thought she needed and might be required to wear to various functions. She had enough knowledge of Caleb's world from her days in London and the various social occasions Tom had forced her to attend—again all in the name of his precious bogus family solidarity.

The concierge had been informed of her arrival and gave her a key before telling her he'd follow her up with the bags. Maggie couldn't stop the unwelcome train of her thoughts as she rode up in the lift—Caleb's catastrophic arrival back into her life was a bitter catalyst precipitating unhappy memories.

She had grown up seeing Tom Holland do his worst to everyone around him—wheeling, dealing, wrecking lives. She had come to hate that world and what it represented. In a way she knew that was one reason why she'd chosen art college—apart from having a unique gift inherited from her father, it had made Tom apoplectic with rage.

She had always avoided him and his cronies like the plague…until those two weeks six months ago. It was only for her mother, otherwise she wouldn't have had anything to do with helping Holland host two weeks of intense meetings and negotiations in his own house. Caleb Cameron had been the guest of honour, invited under the guise of sharing information with some of the world's best financial minds. When all along Tom had planned it in order to get Caleb close… close enough to bring him down.

Maggie had walked straight into the lion's den when she'd seen Caleb for the first time and had fallen head over heels. Not like Tom's usual associates, he'd stood out immediately. Physically and intellectually. And, she'd thought—morally. But how wrong that naïve notion had been. He'd been the same as Tom all along, the same beast in different clothes. But that hadn't stopped the intense attraction flaring.

Unfortunately, Tom had also been aware of the spark that had erupted between them and, with evil cunning, had manipulated events to make sure they were thrown together at every opportunity, all designed to culminate in that night.

The lift doors opened abruptly, ending her intense reverie. She shook herself out of dwelling on the past. She had to think of the future now, surviving for the next eight weeks and then putting as much space between her and Caleb Cameron as possible. She entered the apartment cautiously, walking in and out of the rooms as though they might bite. Nothing but the best, of course, for the city's most venerated guest.

Maggie had read all about this building, this apartment, which had been designed by a world-renowned architect. It stood on a hill opposite the main cathedral and had invited controversy because it represented, some people thought, a jarring juxtaposition to the ancient cathedral across the road. Personally, Maggie loved it. The old facing the new.

She left one room till last, then took a deep breath and opened the door. Much like his office, Caleb's bedroom had wall-to-wall, ceiling-to-floor windows, affording what was truly a millionaire's view of the city. There weren't any personal effects that she could see; a few of Caleb's things were neatly hung in a walk-in dressing room and there were toiletries in the bathroom, but she guessed he hadn't had much time to move in.

Just enough time to take a mistress...

She tried to avoid looking at the focal point, but couldn't. A huge king-size bed dominated the room. Dressed in dark, luxurious linen, it looked crisp and inviting, yet very, very scary. Suddenly an image formed of her with Caleb, limbs entangled, the sheets cast aside, covering her whole body with his own, dark against pale.

What would it be like? Skin to skin...Caleb pressing down on her with his aroused body...

A sound at the door nearly made her jump out of her skin. She whirled around, her hand going to her throat in fright. It was the concierge. The relief that pulsed through her body made her feel weak.

'This is the last of the bags.'

'Thank you so much; you shouldn't have...' She followed the man out and, when he was gone, leant back against the front door, her heart still hammering. Shaking her head, she pushed herself away and set about exploring more thoroughly and putting the clothes in the dressing room.

By nine o'clock that night Maggie's nerves were wound to a stretching point she hadn't known they'd possessed. Every time a noise sounded she held her breath, only relaxing once it had gone away. She'd rung her mother to check in, being as vague as possible about her situation. To her utter relief, she sounded so much improved that Maggie knew she could relax for the first time in a long time. With a friend from the village checking in every day, she knew she'd get a call immediately if anything was wrong.

The phone rang, startling her out of her thoughts. Warily she picked it up.

'Maggie…' A pulse between her legs throbbed just at the sound of his voice; why did it have to come down the line like a caress? She pressed her legs together fiercely.

'Caleb. I was just hoping you weren't in a hospital somewhere.'

She could have sworn she almost heard a chuckle, disconcerting her for a moment. 'I just bet you were. I meant to ring earlier but I've been held up waiting for a call from Los Angeles. With the time difference, I won't get in till after midnight. You should go to bed.'

She remembered how late it had been last night when he'd left the office and bizarrely couldn't stop a rush of concern, which she rapidly dampened. She was disconcerted and flummoxed by his having the courtesy to call.

'I'll go ahead and eat, then.' The minute the words were out, she cursed silently. The last thing she wanted was to appear in any way concerned. Or that she'd been waiting for him.

'Don't tell me you cooked us a romantic meal?'

'No such luck,' she said sweetly, mentally crossing her fingers for the white lie. 'I've been known to burn water.' She had actually prepared a simple casserole, but wasn't going to tell him that.

'I assume you've settled in.'

'Yes.'

'Good. I'll try not to wake you when I get in…or you could always wait up…?'

Maggie faked a yawn, her stomach cramping with panic. 'Much as I'd love to, I can't stay awake. All the excitement… Goodbye, then.'

She was about to put the phone down when she heard her

name; she lifted it back up. His voice was low and lethally silky in her ear. 'If you're not in my bed when I get in, Maggie…you will be by morning.'

The phone clicked down. Maggie thought of the furthest guest room she'd already picked in some futile attempt to deny what was expected of her. She knew he would do exactly as he said. He would carry her bodily out of that bed, into his own.

Knowing she had no choice, she packed away her comfy nightshirt and closed the door on that room. She went into the dressing room, where she'd laid out all the new clothes. She'd placed the underwear and negligées in a drawer. They'd not been her choice to buy, but the shop assistant who'd helped her had been so enthusiastic she hadn't had the heart to curtail her, or deny her the commission. And she thought of a couple of dresses that the girl had picked out. Dresses Maggie would never normally choose…but, she'd guessed at the time, they were dresses that would be suitable for Caleb's mistress to wear. So she had taken them also.

And, if she was honest, a part of her had thought, *Hang Caleb, he can pay for all this ten times over, and more.* She resolutely refused to look too deeply into the possibility that she had in fact bought them because she *wanted* to…for him. She had to remember she was playing a part. And what he would expect was a mistress, dressed suitably, in his bed. That thought made her shiver as she prepared.

Later, while waiting for sleep to claim her, as she lay on the very edge of the huge bed, Maggie reflected uncomfortably that their phone conversation earlier had been almost…too easy, with a hint of warmth even. And that was dangerous. Because it reminded her of the heady days when she'd first got to know him in London, when she'd seen that other side to him. She turned over and rested her head on her hand. If he was to turn on the charm she'd be lost, for certain. She knew because she'd been lost before. Despite everything that had transpired, she was very much afraid that she was still lost.

The drama of the last few days caught up with her finally, the sleepless nights. She gave in to a deep dreamless sleep.

Caleb woke early. He was aware of the heat of another body close to his. Turning so that he was on one side, he looked to see Maggie nestling close, curled towards him. Vibrant red hair fanned out around her head. He'd been dimly aware of her shape on the far side of the bed the previous night and had been too exhausted to investigate further. But they'd obviously gravitated towards each other during the night.

Now, however, he could study her at leisure. She looked younger, innocent…oddly vulnerable. His face took on a hardness as he dismissed the notion, his eyes travelling down. With the cover drawn back, she was revealed in a creamy negligée, the delicate lace just disguising the mounds of her breasts, which rose and fell with even breaths. Caleb felt his body respond forcefully. He shifted uncomfortably and Maggie shifted too, as if they were linked by an invisible thread. He stilled.

In repose, her lips went into what looked almost like a petulant moue. He wanted to bend his head and kiss her soft mouth. He wanted to have her wake and look at him with sleepy eyes, smile and turn into him, giving herself to him. But he didn't. Because he knew that if he was to wake her with a kiss, she'd look at him first with surprise, but then with censure…and, without wanting to question why, he knew he didn't want that. When he made love to her he wanted her eyes to be open, aware of every moment and darkened with passion—when he took her for the first time.

In a split second she had shifted and moved even closer, a hand reaching out, finding his chest and resting there. As if to test him. Small and pale against the darkness of his skin. Fingers curling softly. His jaw clenched with the effort not to give in to temptation and very gently and slowly he extricated himself and went to take a shower. A cold one. On the bed behind him Maggie stirred but did not wake.

CHAPTER FOUR

WHEN Maggie did wake it took a minute to figure out where she was. She felt completely refreshed, as though she'd had the most restorative sleep in her life. Stretching under the covers, she smiled to herself and then stopped. The feel of the slinky silk material on her body was all too alien.

She remembered exactly where she was.

Sitting up slightly, she realised that she was practically on the other side of the bed to the one she'd taken last night and the evidence of a head imprint very close to hers told her that Caleb had joined her at some stage, but he was gone now. From where she was, she must have been on top of him…or maybe he had pulled her over? No, she would have woken. And how had she had such a good sleep with him in the bed beside her? She was a finicky sleeper at the best of times and yet, her first night in a new place, sharing her bed with the most disturbing person she'd ever met, she'd slept like a baby for the first time in years.

The door opened to reveal a clean-shaven, impeccably dressed Caleb. Maggie sank back down and pulled the covers to her chin, unbelievably relieved to see him fully clothed.

'Morning.' He put a cup of coffee on the bedside table. She looked at him very warily.

'You know you're quite the wriggler when you're asleep. All over me when I woke up. You'd think a king-size bed would be big enough…'

Just after the way her own thoughts had been going, it was too much. She would not let him goad her and stifled a defensive retort, but then had to say something.

'Well, maybe this has been a mistake after all, if I slept through the magnitude of sharing your bed without my clothes inadvertently dropping off…'

He came down on the bed beside her and suddenly she couldn't breathe, the air trapped in her throat. Two strong, sinewy arms came either side of her. The sheet slipped down to reveal her upper body, hardly concealed by the lace and satin. His eyes made a leisurely inspection from her face downwards, until his eyes rested on her breasts. Just under his look, she could feel them swell, her nipples tightening into small hard peaks, pouting flagrantly forward, as if begging for his touch. Almost carelessly, he lifted the back of his hand and brushed knuckles over one sensitive peak, causing her to swallow a moan, before he tipped up her chin, forcing her to meet his gaze.

'Mistake…? I don't think so, my love.'

Her insides quivered, her lower body on fire with need. He had proved with little more than a look just how, if he'd wanted to, he could have had her last night, over and over. He knew it and she knew it.

In one fluid movement he stood up from the bed, his expression unreadable. 'I'll be back for you at eleven to go to Monte Carlo, so be ready.'

And he was gone.

Maggie shut her eyes fiercely. She *would* do this. She *had* to. How hard could it be?

* * *

At the designated time Maggie was waiting with a bag, ready to go. She'd rung her mother, had explained that as Caleb's 'assistant' she had to accompany him on a short trip. Having packed away all of her own clothes and dressed in the new ones, she felt a little more like the actress she was trying to be. A simple linen skirt, silk camisole and matching jacket. Her hair twisted back and up in a smart chignon. The phone rang. It was Caleb informing her that he was downstairs in the car. This was it.

Outside, Maggie stood on the steps for a moment. Caleb was watching from the shadows in the back of the car. When she appeared at the door, looking fresh and bright and so sweetly sexy, he had to restrain himself from jumping out to go over and touch her. Almost to see if she was real.

With her bag deposited in the boot seconds later, about to get in Maggie suddenly remembered something and stepped back.

Caleb's voice from the interior was terse. 'What's wrong?'

'I just want to make sure my car is locked…' She hurried over to the car, which was close by, and checked quickly. When she turned to go back, Caleb was standing by the car, shades on against the sun.

'*That* thing is your car?'

'Yes,' she replied defensively.

'It's a health hazard.'

Maggie fought against the protective urge that kicked in. She'd bought that car with her first savings, from the family gardener. She'd learnt to drive in it, lovingly cared for it. She realised then that Caleb, of course, would have expected her to be driving something much more ostentatious. She picked her words carefully, hoping she sounded breezy and uncon-cerned. 'Oh…it's just something I borrow from the house when I'm home. It used to belong to the gardener. It gets me from A to B.'

She slid into his car and hoped he'd forget about it. The driver turned around in his seat to face Maggie, introducing himself as John. She was surprised to hear an English accent. 'Great cars, aren't they? My first was a Mini too. I know how attached you can get to them.' He winked back at her and, with the first genuine human warmth in days, Maggie smiled effervescently back. Then flicked a glance to where Caleb was lounging on the other side of the car.

He was looking at her with a strange expression on his face. She hurriedly schooled her features and looked out of the window. She could see from the corner of her eye when he buried himself in a paper. Without his eyes on her, Maggie breathed slowly and her thoughts for the first time flew ahead to where they were going.

Somewhere warm…and glamorous…and exotic…and foreign. Where the inevitable would happen. Within hours. By the time they got back to Dublin, they were going to be lovers. Her loose top felt constrictive all of a sudden. Could she make love to him and cut herself off from her emotions?

She'd have to.

Maggie lifted her face to the sun. Bliss. If you didn't count the fact that she was here more or less under duress, for which she only had herself to blame, and that her stomach was in a constant knot since Caleb had walked back into her life just three days ago. Her mind reeled at that thought. Three days…and now she was about to start the life of a kept woman with someone who despised her…yet desired her enough to look past it.

She opened her eyes and shaded them against the sun. She was sitting out on the terrace of their hotel suite, on a balcony that overlooked a small idyllic square. Flowers everywhere burst in a colourful profusion so bright that it almost hurt the eye. She got up and leant against the wall. The sea glinted and sparkled in the distance. How many other women had had this treatment? Whisked away at a moment's notice to luxurious hotels, fantastic locations… there purely for *his* pleasure. The thought hurt like a knife edge in her heart and she angrily pushed herself away from the wall.

She gave a startled gasp when she saw Caleb lounging against the French window that led back into the suite. His eyes were shaded.

'How long have you been there…? What happened to your meeting?' She felt absurdly exposed, as though he'd known exactly what she'd been thinking about.

He pushed himself away from the door and walked over. 'You should be careful…you'll burn in this sun.' He could already see that more freckles had appeared on her face and shoulders, making her look ridiculously young.

She stiffened under his finger as it trailed over the smooth skin of her shoulder, hoping he wouldn't see how she was responding to the light touch. 'Don't worry,' she said breezily, belying her tense body. 'Many painful past experiences have made sure that I never go out unless I've got factor thirty on. I gave up trying to tan years ago.'

He was still caressing her hot skin. 'Still…you should watch out.'

'If you're not careful, I might think you are concerned for my welfare,' she mocked.

Caleb's mouth thinned. 'Hardly. You come with an expensive price tag. And I don't intend waiting for you to recover from sunstroke tonight.'

Her mouth went dry. Despite his blatant insult, she couldn't halt the images that invaded her head at the thought of *tonight*. She searched for words, something to negate the awful liquid heat that was winding its way through her blood, glad that his eyes were covered so she couldn't see into the blue depths, where she could well imagine his contempt laid bare.

He spoke before she could articulate a word. 'My first meeting was quicker than I thought. I haven't eaten yet; have you?'

She shook her head.

'I've got a table in a bistro just around the corner; let's get something light, I have another meeting in about an hour.'

'Okay…' Maggie picked up her bag and followed him out of the suite. A short stroll from the hotel and tucked down a small cobbled side street, Caleb gestured to a restaurant artfully hidden by plants and flowering baskets. Inside, it was cool and airy. The waiter led them to an intimate table in the corner beside an open window.

It was romantic and glamorous beyond belief. Heady stuff, with Caleb across the small table, long legs stretched out alongside hers. When she realised that, she tucked hers primly under her chair. He noted her movement with a mocking lift of one brow. She ignored it.

He handed her a menu. The waiter came back and they gave their order, Caleb asking for some sparkling water. When the waiter left the water and had gone again, Caleb lifted his glass. 'In the absence of wine…can we drink to a truce, Maggie?'

A fluttery feeling hit her belly. She couldn't avoid his eyes, the blue hypnotising her. She lifted her glass too, dampening the feeling ruthlessly. He was doing this just to make things easier for himself. No one wanted a reluctant mistress. And she *had* to stop her wayward thoughts… 'To a truce, then…'

He smiled. She took a sip and the rogue fluttery feeling came back a thousandfold. When he trained that smile on her…she couldn't think straight. Danger.

*He's turning on the charm, just to get what he wants— you…*a little sing-song voice warned. Maggie ignored it. She knew exactly what he was doing.

'Let's not forget why we're here though…'

'Enlighten me, Maggie, please.' A hard glitter entered his eyes.

'The house, of course.'

'Ah, yes. The house. I was attempting, however hopelessly, to give us the chance to perhaps ignore the ugly reality. You don't need to remind me of how you're bartering yourself for a house worth millions. The fact is you are. And I'm the fool who thinks you're worth it.' His words rang with bitterness and she could see a pulse beat at his temple. He obviously regretted saying too much.

She flushed a dull red. Well, she'd asked for it. And why did she feel in the wrong? Just because he was the one who had held out the tentative olive branch?

She took a gulp of water.

He leant forward. 'But Maggie, there's no reason why we can't come to some mutual accord.'

She had to be careful; she was letting her vulnerable emotions run away with her. The type of woman he was used to wouldn't bat an eyelid at what they were doing. She strove for that cool insouciance. Albeit slightly after the fact.

'Yes. You're right. Let's drink to that truce again.' She held up her glass. With narrowed, calculating eyes he clinked hers again. She smiled brilliantly, hiding the hurt. She willed the awkward feeling away and, with more aplomb and skill than she'd thought she could possibly possess, she managed to steer them into a light conversation.

As Caleb seemed to disregard her little outburst, as they talked of inconsequential matters, like a bittersweet pain, she remembered all too well how much they'd had in common, or so she had thought. How much she'd loved talking to him once. Without knowing how it happened, somehow they'd gravitated to more personal matters.

'Do you go back to Rio much?' The plates had been cleared and Maggie was cradling her coffee cup in one hand, feeling deliciously full. Even though they hadn't had wine, she felt a mellow feeling snake through her bones, relaxing her. And it surprised her, how easily she'd let herself become this relaxed.

Caleb looked away for a second and something flashed over his face. 'Not that much. Although my mother is still there, she's busy with her new husband…'

'You mentioned him before, didn't you? Isn't he—'

'The same age as me.' He gave a harsh laugh. 'Yes. And he has lots of money for her to be kept in the style to which she's accustomed.'

Maggie tried desperately to keep things light. 'Well, you have to admit, for feminists out there, it's a nice reversal. Usually it's the other way around, an old man with a woman no older than his own daughter.'

There was tension for a second and then Caleb smiled. 'You're right. You'd probably like her, you know. She's very forthright, very outspoken.'

She felt suddenly shy at the thought of meeting his mother, but knew he hadn't meant it like that, literally. If anything, it was more likely to be a cloaked insult.

'Is…is your father still in England?'

He nodded as he took a sip of coffee, 'Yes. He's in Brighton, so I get down there whenever I can.' There was none of the tension in his voice when talking about his father. Maggie guessed he had a very fraught relationship with his mother and remembered him telling her before about how his parents had fought over him as a boy, having divorced when he'd been only three or four. He'd been shunted back and forth between Brazil and the UK for years.

'But you're living in London? Or you were…' She couldn't say the words, *six months ago*.

He nodded briefly. 'I have an apartment there and one in Rio, New York, Paris…but I'm never in one place long enough to call it home…'

At that moment he caught her eyes and they were clouded with some indefinable emotion; it reached out across the table and made him suddenly feel the need for something he'd never felt before. Maggie cut into his disturbing thoughts, echoing them.

'I can't imagine that. All the years we lived in London, Ireland was always our home. Somewhere to come back to…'

A refuge from terror. Dublin had always been too boring for Tom. He'd never stayed long and her happiest times had been during her Irish boarding school years whenever he'd let her mother stay…which had usually been when he was off on a holiday with one of his many mistresses.

'Is that where you'll stay now?'

She dragged her attention back and nodded. 'I'd like to. We've been home for six months—'

'Six months?' He was sharp. Maggie coloured guiltily and wondered frantically if she'd let her guard down too much. But what could that possibly tell him?

She picked her words carefully. 'Mum wanted to come home, so I came back with her to settle her in…'

His eyes were narrowed on her face. Intense. 'So you left London six months ago?'

Maggie nodded.

Caleb studied her. There was a kernel of something there; he was sure of it. But he couldn't figure what it was. Tom must have sent her away, fearing that Caleb might somehow come after her. Protection. The thought made him feel that impotent rage again. At her betrayal, at his own weakness for her. He made a huge effort to put it out of his mind. They'd agreed to a truce. 'You're close to your mother?'

Maggie, relieved that he'd let the London focus go, nodded emphatically. She was unaware of the protective gleam that lit her eyes, making them almost luminous. Caleb's breath stopped; she looked radiant. The sun had already given her pale skin a warm glow, freckles that made him want to reach out and touch. Her top hinted at the valley between her breasts. A tendril of red-gold hair had drifted over one shoulder and curled tantalisingly close to her breast. This was crazy; he felt jealous…of some hair? He shifted on his seat, his body throbbing. Tonight, he vowed, a steady pulse of anticipation and desire beating through his blood…

A short while later, making their way back to the hotel, Caleb casually took Maggie's hand in his. She felt tiny and feminine next to his much larger build. He threaded his fingers through hers and she was on very shaky legs by the time they returned. He turned to face her. She looked up, meeting his eyes. The sun was behind him, dazzling her.

He was going to kiss her and there was nothing she could do to stop it. If she tried…he'd wonder why and that would lead them down a dangerous path. Their mutual attraction was undeniable—always had been. He wouldn't understand her fear… He had her pegged as someone far more sophisticated in these matters. This was a simple transaction for him and no doubt he imagined it was the same for her. She couldn't afford to appear anything less than willing from now on. For as long as he desired her. And she knew that as terrified as she was of the response he evoked in her physically, it was the emotional minefield at the other end that worried her most.

He pulled her close into his body with one arm, his other hand cradling her head and threading through the silky strands of her hair. His mouth touched hers.

With flames of desire licking along every vein, Maggie finally gave in and, for the first time since seeing him again, even though they'd already kissed, she kissed him back. With full consciousness. Because, despite everything, she wanted to. Because she couldn't *not*. This was as necessary to her as breathing. Her mind fought a pathetic battle for a few seconds; it must be the surroundings…the feeling that somehow they were not in the real world, that was making her behave like this… She just couldn't help it.

With a moan of approval, he felt her tacit acquiescence and tightened the embrace. His tongue sought hers and sweetly stroked and explored and plundered. Maggie gave into powerful desire and slid her hands up his arms. She could feel the bunched muscle under the thin material of his shirt and desperately wanted to be able to feel the silky skin, explore the texture of his muscles, feel how they shifted…changed contours as he held her.

When he finally lifted his head, he pressed another quick kiss to her mouth as though he was loath to let her go. Maggie felt dizzy and light-headed. The only thing holding her upright was his arm anchoring her to him. She hated herself for this; he had her exactly where he wanted her. Acquiescent and pliant, in his arms. And there was nothing she could do except…comply.

'I won't have much time later so I'll have my tux delivered to me and meet you in the hotel bar before the function.' He let her go and pushed her gently in the direction of the hotel. Before she could be completely humiliated, she turned and briskly walked into the hotel, without a backward glance.

CHAPTER FIVE

DISMISSING the car and deciding to walk back to his meeting, which was just a few minutes away, Caleb's mind raced. That kiss…and Maggie filled his senses so much that the thought of work was a thorn in his side. His step became more brisk, as if he could put distance between himself and his uncomfortable thoughts. He'd had other mistresses, lots…what was the problem now? Maggie was just another one. Then he remembered reluctantly that, walking down a street in London some weeks before and seeing the back of a petite redhead, his pulse had quickened through his body with such force that he'd been shaking by the time he'd caught up with her, only to find that she was nothing like Maggie. The force of need that had ripped through him had disturbed him more than he'd cared to admit at the time.

Was that what had spurred him to see her again? To wreak the final, devastating revenge? Because he hated the pull she still had over him?

He berated himself inwardly for giving rein to such thoughts. Applied the stern logic he was famed for. He desired her and she'd offered him the key he'd needed to make her his mistress, *that was all*. She was just the next in line, however she'd come to him. Reluctantly or not. And the jury was still out on whether or not she had manipulated events from the word go. She had, after all, been instrumental in a bid to see him crushed. He could never afford to forget that. Could never trust her.

But now, after just hours in Maggie's company—a woman who didn't even pretend to like him—for the first time ever he was suddenly wishing for an afternoon off. Why on earth was he suddenly questioning the control he wielded that didn't make it easy for him to walk away on a whim? It was desire pure and simple. Even if it was a more powerful desire than he'd ever experienced, still, that's all it was. Nothing else. Yet…

Yet nothing…

He hated the thought that he could very well be dancing to her tune…still.

As she waited that evening for the lift to arrive, Maggie's reflection stared back from the mirrored door. She felt a little unrecognisable. Having always rebelled at Tom's attempts to get her to 'dress-up', she had never normally made much of an effort.

And yet now…she suddenly felt the urge? a small mocking voice jeered in her ear. Still, she was glad she'd made the effort, she told herself defiantly, pressing the button again with undue force, a quiver of butterflies taking flight in her belly when the bell pinged loudly, announcing the lift's arrival.

Caleb nursed a whiskey in the dark bar as he waited. He drew admiring, openly covetous looks from every woman there. He knew it, could feel it, was always aware of it, but let it roll off him like droplets of water off a duck's back. The only gaze he sought right now was a green-eyed one. Except it was more likely to be combative than covetous, despite her acquiescence earlier.

He was steeled to see her again. All defences raised. She'd

invaded his thoughts all afternoon, had made him lose his concentration, his focus. He'd found himself on the verge of agreeing to a merger that would have cost him millions until he'd woken up at the last moment. This is what she'd done before. And, after the call he'd just taken from his assistant in Dublin, he knew she was up to a lot more than wanting her house back for her poor, *supposedly* innocent, mother. She was up to a whole lot more.

A distinct hush fell over the already muted tones of conversation in the bar. The hairs stood up on the back of Caleb's neck as he looked up slowly from his glass. Maggie stood in the doorway. His chest grew tight and his breathing constricted as he drank in the sight of her. She looked…stunning.

He could see her eyes dart around the room and knew she wouldn't see him straight away as he was partially hidden, a force of habit. She wore a dark olive-coloured dress, the flowing folds meeting in a deep V over an empire-line that rested just under her bosom, the pale voluptuous swells hinting at other hidden curves. Her hair was held back from one side and swept over her other shoulder in a thick russet wave. She stood out from every other woman there, with their overdone, overtight bodies and faces. Like a glowing pearl against dark coral.

His hand tightened reflexively on the glass when her gaze caught his and an immediate flush of colour entered her cheeks. She moved towards him and for a split second he had the strongest urge to leave, run…get away. As if he was on a collision course with a very definite yet unknown danger.

And then she stopped in front of him and he was still there. She looked up at him, the almond shape of her eyes accentuated with kohl and a clean, fresh scent which intoxicated his nostrils. He summoned all of his skill and experience to bring the guard down over his conflicting emotions. He stood. 'If you're ready, let's go.'

Maggie searched his face for some clue of what he was thinking but could see nothing. He hadn't even said if he thought she looked okay. He took her hand possessively and led her out to the foyer entrance, where a sleek car pulled up and he guided her into the back before following. Back in the bar he'd been so brusque she hadn't had a chance to get her breath, since it had been taken by the sight of him. But now she took him in surreptitiously. He was even more handsome in the tuxedo, his hair smoothed back, highlighting the strong forehead, the aquiline line of his nose.

But he didn't look happy. After hesitating for a moment, she couldn't help asking, 'Is…is everything okay?'

He shot her a brooding look.

'You just seem a little preoccupied…is it work?'

'What's this?' he sneered. 'The nice, caring, considerate Maggie? Trying to lull me into a false sense of security… charm me?'

'What are you talking about?'

Caleb knew he was being irrational and that he was reacting to something he wasn't even aware of, but couldn't stop. He wanted to push Maggie back to a safe distance.

'You must have known I was close to bringing Holland to his knees—he certainly did. I don't trust you for a second. I know you're up to something more than trying to secure the house.'

Maggie quailed at the contempt stamped into his features and a sharp pain filled her chest because she had known no such thing and she trembled with the effort not to cry tears of frustration. 'It's not bad enough that you believe me to have betrayed you once—now you're trying to accuse me of more?'

'Absolutely.' His tone rang with conviction. 'And if you

think that by taking you as my mistress it will afford you that opportunity, then you'd better wise up fast.'

Maggie was genuinely aghast. Where had this come from? As if reading her thoughts, he answered her question. He leaned over and took her hands, dragging her close to his chest. His scent enveloped her and Maggie closed her eyes in a futile attempt to avoid his sensual threat.

'You think you're smart, do you? To spend such a small amount of money on the clothes…then making sure I see the ancient car, as though you wouldn't normally be driving something much more expensive.'

Her eyes snapped open. Wide. 'What?'

Had he lost his mind?

'All designed, no doubt, to make me think that perhaps I've judged you too harshly…'

'That's crazy…' His words cut her to the quick. Too close to the bone. Of course he would have checked up on her. She thought of the amount of money she'd put on his account; it had taken a lot of nerve to walk away with her head high. What on earth was he used to? She shook her head. 'Maybe I'm just different to your other—'

'Different? I don't think so, Maggie; they're always upfront about what they want. Honest. You're conniving and deceitful.'

His words were hurting her in a place she didn't want to look at. She fought back.

'And maybe you're just too cynical.'

He smiled grimly, still in possession of her hands, 'You could say that. My mother taught me that all women appreciate the spoils of being a rich man's plaything and I've yet to meet a woman to persuade me otherwise… Perhaps it's your mother who has taken on Tom's legacy, thinking you can both manipulate me, using you as the bait again. Is that why she couldn't meet me that day at the house…? You were laying the ground work for the sympathy vote even then, getting Murphy to tell me she was weakened by everything…'

At the mention of her mother, Maggie stiffened against his hands, her face paling dramatically. Her voice shook with emotion. 'Don't you ever mention my mother like that again. This is between you and me. That's all you need to know; keep her out of this.'

Caleb took in her passionate response. She seemed genuinely angry. He kept holding her, his eyes trying to assess the expressions flitting across her face. But then the moment was gone… He saw her face close up again.

Maggie couldn't take back the words and knew she'd given far too much away. But she couldn't bear to think of her mother being so slighted. It made her sick that he could even think that for a second. Miserably she knew she couldn't say anything, make him listen to her. She couldn't defend herself anyway—that way lay exposure to ridicule and betraying her mother's secret pain.

So instead she pasted a brilliant smile on her face and tossed her head, praying that he wouldn't dwell on her careless words. She had to be more careful.

'As for the clothes, I only got what I needed for now…and what's wrong with hoping for a few spoils…after all, I am your plaything for the next two months, am I not? Unless, of course, you want to let me go? If what I am is too distasteful to you—'

With a sudden harsh breath that was expelled heavily, Caleb silenced her words with his mouth. And, as much as Maggie's own self-respect screamed at her to pull away, shout out her innocence, she felt herself moulding into Caleb's chest, her soft curves pressing into rock-hard muscle. Her senses quickly became drunk on him, but suddenly the car came to a smooth halt, not that she would have even noticed if Caleb hadn't pulled back at that moment. His eyes glittered fiercely in the dim light as they waited for the door to be opened.

'Just don't forget that that's all you are, Maggie. My plaything.'

The heat of the ballroom was stifling, even with all the doors thrown open to the fragrant night outside. Maggie's cheeks ached and the balls of her feet were burning in the high heels. She was moving from foot to foot in an effort to ease the pain. Caleb, at her side, looked down sharply.

'What's wrong with you?'

She refused to look at him, staring at a point to his left. 'Nothing.' She'd barely communicated with him since they'd arrived, still stung and hurt and dismayed by the level of his distrust.

He hadn't seemed to even notice. For what seemed like hours now, she'd endured conversations of inane small talk, being relegated to the sidelines while Caleb had entertained a never ending stream of sycophantic admirers. And she'd endured none too friendly speculative glances from every other woman in the room. When a crush of people had moved forward, Maggie had got separated from Caleb and found herself surrounded by three or four women. They were all dressed in what she knew to be haute couture, totally over the top, but a clear statement of their wealth and status. They had looked her up and down as if she were a specimen in a glass box. She couldn't believe how rude they were being and tried not to look as intimidated as she felt. One of them spoke.

'Vous êtes ici avec Monsieur Cameron?'

Without even thinking, Maggie immediately slipped into her schoolgirl French, trying to be polite, wondering who they were and why they wanted to know. *'Oui…'*

'Ah, bon. Mais juste pour ce soir, n'est ce pas?'

Maggie was trying to figure out what the woman was saying… Was she actually suggesting that she was here with Caleb just for tonight, like some kind of…call girl? A mortified blush rushed through her; they were hemming her in and their overdone faces, lacquered hair and cloying perfume was making her feel sick.

'I'm sorry…excuse me.' She tried to push her way out, but couldn't. She was feeling more and more desperate.

Caleb swivelled his head. Where had she gone? She'd been at his side only two minutes before. He'd got caught in a conversation with a property investor from France and hadn't been able to extricate himself. He felt mildly guilty that he hadn't been more attentive to Maggie, but he was still feeling the uncomfortable sensation of being somehow open, foolish in his desire for her… He had to be careful around her.

Then he saw her. She was surrounded by the doyennes of Monte Carlo—he knew them well. His mouth tightened. They were responsible for many matchmaking attempts with one or other of their invariably too young, spoilt and petulant daughters. And he suddenly realised that Maggie looked terrified. Without stopping to think, and knowing that it surprised him as he would have imagined her to be a match for them, he strode over and reached through the women to take Maggie's arm.

She looked up and the flash of sheer relief and something else that crossed her face made something flip flop in his chest. But then it was gone, as if it had never happened, and now her eyes flashed veritable sparks at him. He smiled his excuses to the ladies and led Maggie away.

'Are you okay?' He slanted a look down at her.

She glared up at him. 'No thanks to you. Those women are...unbelievable.' She shook her head. 'You could have warned me I'd need a flak jacket to come here.'

He couldn't help the unbidden smile. He doubted the women would last again in Maggie's company; they'd obviously just caught her off guard. He could well imagine what they'd said. And again he wondered at how she hadn't been better able to handle them. He would have cast her as one herself—well used to the poison-talon-tipped women of society who were more akin to social climbing piranhas.

He refused to dwell on that now. He was thinking ahead and wondering how long he could suffer to be polite before he could get out of there and take Maggie with him. Take her to bed.

'Ah Cameron, there you are...'

Not just yet, anyway. He pulled Maggie into his side, swallowed a grimace and smiled as yet another colleague bore down on him.

Maggie flicked the object of everyone's fascination a reluctant look, anger still bubbling through her. She had to admit that he *was* the most handsome man in the room. He stood head and shoulders above everyone and with that physique...again her insides cramped with nerves and anticipation. Finally, after what seemed like more torturous hours, he leant down, his mouth close to her ear, sending a little shock wave through her.

'Let's get out of here.'

She nodded mutely. Time was up, no more waiting. Tonight he would demand payment...take her body and, she was afraid, her soul too. And she couldn't say a thing.

She suddenly felt absurdly vulnerable and alone, her anger dissolving. What *could* she say, anyway? As she followed him through the crowd, stopping every two seconds for people to say goodbye, she thought a little hysterically of what she might say if given a chance: how six months ago, on the day of their date, Tom, her beloved stepfather had informed her of his plans to take Caleb over and ruin him. And how, if Maggie didn't co-operate with his plans to keep Caleb *occupied*, he would beat Maggie's mother so comprehensively that—in Tom's succinct, devastating words, 'I'll put her in hospital'.

She could tell him how she'd racked her brains for a way out…but had known, no matter what she did, even if she'd gone to the police, that he'd still make her mother pay. Because, you see, he'd been doing it for years. Once, in her youthful naïvety, Maggie *had* gone to the police. Tom hadn't punished *her*… No, it had been her mother who'd suffered, even though she'd claimed a random mugging to protect Tom. Classic bullying, abusive tactics. He had been very cunning—you could never see the bruises. They had always been well hidden.

She could tell him of how, before Tom's bombshell, she'd been ridiculously excited at the thought of going on the date with him, had even bought a new outfit. But then…that was when Tom had forced her to go to that shop, had bought that excuse for a dress instead. And had informed her of her role in his awful macabre play.

She could tell him how she'd been so filled with guilt that she couldn't go through with sleeping with him, that was why she'd stopped… She'd been on the verge of actually telling him everything, somehow trusting that, maybe for once, her mother could be protected.

Maggie was not in Monte Carlo any more; she was back in that hotel room, the memories rushing back with sickening clarity, and she was powerless to escape them. She was on that bed, the sheet pulled around her shaking, half naked body as Caleb stood in front of her, pulling on his clothes. 'Maggie, you're a fool. You think I didn't know exactly what you had planned?' He gave a harsh laugh as he pulled on his shirt. Maggie felt an icy stream washing through her, the defensive words of explanation dying on her lips.

'I heard your stepfather. His exact words were, "That stepdaughter of mine will do anything and she wants Cameron; she's with us". So you see, Maggie, I've known for days now that you've been cooking up this little plan…very hammy, though. And the outfit? I've seen classier ones on women who tout for business on the streets.'

Maggie could feel her insides contracting, pulling inward as if to protect herself from the cruel blows. Her voice was dry and raspy when it came out. 'But…I never knew…I—'

'Save it, Maggie. You knew all right. I even have the evidence.'

And she watched as he found his jacket and took out a small envelope, throwing the contents at her. Photos. Lots of them—of Tom and her on Oxford Street, going into the shop, emerging with the bag. Getting into his car. And from these deceptive angles it looked to all the world as though she were the eager accomplice…

She looked up with huge wounded eyes, 'But when, how…?'

He was almost dressed, not even looking at her any more. 'I had you followed for the day, just to see for myself. And what a pretty picture those photos paint, don't you think?'

'But…you've known…you knew all along, for the past—'

'Yes, Maggie, I've known since practically the first day we met. So all those shy, innocent glances, the blushes, were for nothing. Entertaining, but for nothing.'

'But how could you, I mean, why did you…do it?' She

didn't know why she was still speaking, couldn't understand what protective part of her hadn't kicked in yet.

He came close to the bed and she had to look up. His face was coldly impassive. Shut. 'Because, Maggie, I desired you. I wanted you. And I knew I could have you. You were offering yourself on a plate, for God's sake…' He came down close to her, hands on either side of her body, where she could see the utter disgust and contempt in his eyes. 'We both know I could still have you now…' he flicked a derisory glance up and down '…but I can't be bothered. Because, believe me, I never want to see your face again.'

And he walked out of the room without a backward glance. Maggie sat on the bed for a long time, the cold seeping into her bones as she felt something within her shrivel up and die.

By now they were at the entrance to the function room but Maggie wasn't even aware. She was locked in her own private hell of memories. Caleb looked abstractedly at her hand in his—it was icy cold. Then he looked at her face. She was so pale that he felt a jolt go through him. When he called her name she didn't respond. Something was very wrong. He lifted her into his arms and strode out of the building. In the car he held her close to his body. He knew that, whatever it was, she wasn't faking it. No one could fake that.

Back at the hotel, he carried her again, all the way from the car up to the suite. Once inside he poured a glass of brandy and sat her down, making her swallow it. He could see the effect of the alcohol hitting her system; her eyes flared and she coughed. And then she started to shake uncontrollably. He pulled her into his body, waiting until the shaking subsided. Finally he could feel her pull away slightly and he let her go. She looked at him as though seeing him for the first time.

'What…what happened?'

She could see a light of rare concern in his eyes and wondered faintly what had put it there, while also having the wits to wish desperately that he was *really* concerned for her.

He brushed her hair back with a gesture that was almost tender, confusing her even more. 'I think you fainted…without fainting. I've seen it before. It's like a state of shock.'

Maggie dimly remembered following him out of the function room but for the life of her couldn't remember anything else. She shook her head. 'I don't know why… I'm sorry…'

'Don't be,' he said abruptly. 'Why don't you get ready for bed? You should sleep.'

She nodded her head and went into the bathroom. She felt exhausted, as if she'd run a marathon.

Caleb went out to the balcony and stood leaning on the same wall that Maggie had earlier. He shook his head. How could she be feeling such grief for that odious man? For that was what it was, *must be*. Yet, for all that she was, all that her stepfather had been, he shouldn't have underestimated the fact that she was bound to be in mourning. They had been family, after all. His cynical brain kicked into gear. Perhaps it was also the delayed shock of finding out that Tom's millions weren't going to be hers after all. That thought made something cold settle into his chest.

He went to the door of the suite and looked in. Maggie lay curled up on the bed, already asleep.

CHAPTER SIX

WHEN she woke the next morning Maggie's head throbbed. She was alone in the bed. A note on the pillow next to her caught her eye:

I'm at a meeting but will come and meet you for lunch on the terrace at twelve-thirty. Caleb.

She checked the bedside clock. It was ten a.m. Sinking back on to the pillows, fragments of the previous night came back. Like water dripping into a well, she began to recall what had made her have that bizarre, terrifying reaction. She remembered the crowds, the heat of the room and then how her thoughts had begun to circulate sickeningly on the events of all those months before.

She had to concede that it was possible for a kind of delayed shock to set in. She'd been shouldering the burden for so long…even her mother didn't know what had happened in London, the extent of Maggie's involvement. The threat that only Maggie had been aware of.

And her mother wasn't even aware of the plans Maggie had made for them to flee and hide in case Tom came after them. How relieved she'd been when she'd managed to persuade her mother to return home. Because she'd known that Tom would soon find out that Caleb had been aware all along, had prepared for the crude takeover bid. And when he found out, she knew he'd have blamed her…she worried her lower lip…but what had obviously happened then was that Caleb had immediately launched his own retaliation, thereby keeping Tom occupied. In a sick, twisted way, she recognised now that he had inadvertently saved her and her mother from Tom's wrath.

It had to be seeing Caleb again, all the intense emotions he was provoking…that had led to a mini meltdown of sorts. She managed to smile ruefully at herself as she went on to the terrace to soak up the morning sun; she'd never seen herself as a drama queen.

Then she remembered how gentle Caleb had been, how he'd held her tight against his body. A warmth invaded her limbs; she could still recall the feeling of safety. The yearning that had overwhelmed her with its sweetness. The wish that it could be for real… She was very much afraid of being sucked into the same dangerous dream as before. A dream of Caleb *loving* her. She blocked the thought ruthlessly and went inside to have a shower. She didn't love him…she didn't. She didn't even like him.

But you thought you did once… Can you just switch that off?

She ignored the prompt; if she repeated the words enough to herself like a mantra, she might just believe it.

At twelve-thirty Maggie was feeling back to normal. A table had just been delivered with a mouth-watering array of food—fresh fish, salad and crusty bread and a bottle of champagne on ice. She heard the door in the suite open and close and stood slightly awkwardly on the terrace when Caleb emerged. Her heart tripped predictably, the way it did every time she saw him, whether it had been seconds or hours in the interim.

'How are you this morning?' he asked coolly.

'Fine. Much better. About last night, I'm so sorry, that's never happened before.'

He lifted a hand. 'It's fine.'

'Okay…' Maggie trailed off. He clearly didn't want to discuss it. Maybe he *was* angry that they hadn't slept together. Maybe he thought it was an elaborate attempt on her part to avoid it? She suddenly hated the thought he might suspect that of her. She moved closer and put an impulsive hand on his arm. 'You don't think that I… Well, that I did it on purpose to…' She stopped, her face crimson with awkwardness and a cold horror struck her… *Had* her body somehow shut down because of that too?

'No, of course not.' And he genuinely didn't. That thought had never even entered his head and it surprised him now.

The residue of her disturbing thoughts still lingered and she answered absently, 'Good.'

'Let's eat.'

'All right.'

They sat down at the table that had been erected, complete with a pristine tablecloth and gleaming cutlery. With only the faint sounds of a few cars down in the square, someone calling to someone else, it was unbelievably intimate and private on their little terrace. The scent of the flowers hung heavy in the air.

Caleb busied himself opening the champagne and poured Maggie a glass before tending to himself. She murmured thanks and tried to appear cool, as though this happened every day for her.

'So what's on the cards for later? Another dinner?'

Caleb inclined his head. 'Yes, I'm afraid so. But you don't have to come if you think you're not up to it.'

His consideration touched her, despite the wall of ice she was trying to pack around her heart as she looked at him. She shook her head. 'No, I'll be fine. I'm not normally the fainting type. It's really never happened before.' She even felt guilty now because she knew what had brought it on. Not that she could tell him. She had to make an effort to appear unconcerned. As if he didn't hold her world in his hands.

She flashed him a rare smile. 'I can't wait to fend off more women, listen to people talk about the royal family as though they're intimate friends and try to decipher your financial jargon…'

A sharp burst of empathy made him suck in a breath. He caught himself and grimaced, unable to help a rueful smile that transformed his face and took Maggie's breath away; he seemed to have taken her unspoken cue to be light too. It made him look years younger.

'I'm sorry; I know how boring they can be. As for fending off the women, you saw the worst of the bunch last night. They don't see me, they see dollar signs, no ring and a potential husband for their daughters.'

She was thrown by his apology. He seemed for once not to be lumping her into that category and he was wrong—they saw far more than that. He was all the more attractive because of his youth, virility *and* his wallet. She couldn't help asking, 'Don't you want to get married some day?'

She could feel herself holding her breath as she saw the expressions flit over his face and the shutters came back down. A muscle twitched at his jaw. His voice was unbearably harsh. 'With what I've seen? Hardly. If I do marry, it'll be purely a business arrangement…and for children.'

She couldn't help the shiver that seemed to invade her very bones at his words. In a way, from the brief experience she'd had of the circles he moved in, she couldn't blame him. She remembered the looks of pure vitriol that had come her way from those women and could only imagine the conversations in the bathroom. There was a melancholic ring to his words too that made Maggie want to question him, find out what had put it there, find out more about his life, parents…but she couldn't.

In an effort to avoid talking about anything too personal, she started chattering about anything and everything. Caleb sat back and studied her. She was casual in a sleeveless cross-over top and linen trousers. And something niggled him about that, but before he could figure out what it was, he was distracted. Her face was animated, telling a story, but he was captivated by her movements, the way her eyes widened in emphasising a point. They'd spent two nights sharing the same bed…and still not slept together. That was a first for him. And he knew he couldn't bear to wait much longer. He'd woken several times during the previous night and even had to take a cold shower at one stage. Again.

'…and that was it, really.' Maggie stopped awkwardly; she knew he hadn't really been listening to her. Was she that boring?

Caleb sat forward. 'Sorry, I was miles away.'

'That's okay.' She smiled tightly.

Suddenly he felt like kicking himself. He'd hurt her, by not listening to her. And he was perplexed by her reaction. Shouldn't she be cajoling him now? Making him pay for his lack of attention, sliding on to his lap, trying to entice him to go to bed for the afternoon?

He shook his head. Her act of innocence was so ingrained that it was second nature. He shook his head at himself. She was reeling him in *again*.

'What is it?' Maggie had a look of almost concern on her face.

'Nothing,' he said harshly. He stood and pushed back his chair; it sounded shrill on the stone ground. Maggie flinched, a tiny movement. 'You should take it easy this afternoon.'

She could be cool too. 'I'm fine, Caleb, really. It won't happen again. I'm going to do some sightseeing this afternoon.' She shrugged lightly. 'I might never be back here again…'

His eyes narrowed. She really hadn't said that with any guile. Had she? His mouth quirked dryly. 'Oh, I'm sure you could persuade someone to bring you here again…'

She fought off the urge to defend herself from the obvious implication that he meant another lover…if she could even call him that. Right now, when he was being cynical and hateful, it was very easy to forget nonsensical, fantastical notions of being in love. She clung on to it like a shield around her heart.

'I'm sure you're right.' And she smiled up at him sunnily.

'I'll see you this evening. We go out at half seven.'

She nodded her head and watched as he walked away, sagging back into the chair once he'd gone, only aware then how much tension she'd been holding in.

Maggie was determined that Caleb would not affect her equilibrium, not with thoughts of the evening ahead or his tart barbs. So much for their short-lived truce.

She was doing a bus top sightseeing tour. But…try as she might, she couldn't block out the fantasy that hovered annoyingly like a wispy mist on the periphery of her mind. That if they'd met under different circumstances, he could perhaps feel something for her—beyond the mild contempt, distrust, all wrapped up in overwhelming desire, which was the reality.

She flipped her sunglasses back down on to her nose and

grimaced. That was the problem; even if she could indulge herself for one second that Caleb didn't have an axe to grind with her…then that would only put her in the same category as his usual mistresses. Which meant, she knew well, a bit of fun for a while, being indulged, cosseted, then…he'd walk away. That was what he'd meant last night, when he'd alluded to the fact that they always knew where they stood with him. And, even if that was the case, that wouldn't be enough. Not for her.

Maybe they had thicker skins? She valiantly ignored the absurd desire to line all of them up in front of a firing range. In a way, she reassured herself, she was better off; because she and Caleb had such a tangled history, it meant that he would never allow her to get too close.

Or you him…

Of course! she thought angrily, answering herself, it worked in her favour too. It did. She just wasn't entirely sure how…yet.

She spotted something on the street and got off at the next stop. Without questioning why, she found herself walking into the beautician's she'd seen. It was *not* because she wanted to make an effort. It was *not* giving into this fantasy. It was just female pride.

That night at another glittering function, it was like a carbon copy of the previous night. The same people, the same conversations. And yet…what was going on between them was subtly different. Maggie was tucked into Caleb's side, a possessive arm around her waist. He was including her in conversations, making it very clear she was with him. His woman. She could remember the look he'd given her earlier when she'd emerged from the dressing room in the suite. Her whole body still tingled from it.

At the beauticians she'd been waxed, plucked, buffed.

Nothing that he would notice…but she knew. That somehow made it erotic. She berated herself. Indulging herself like this would only end in pain. She knew it. But she couldn't help it. Couldn't help the devilish, rogue desire within her that had chosen the dress she had. It was one of the ones the sales girl had picked out, something Maggie would never normally have the nerve to wear. But something she guessed would be *suitable*.

With her hair piled in a loose knot on top of her head, the black dress was deceptively simple. A cowl neckline at the front didn't reveal too much but then, behind, it fell away, revealing her whole back. She'd always been self-conscious of her freckles everywhere but somehow now, here with Caleb, with his possessive arm around her, she felt…something close to beautiful for the first time in her life.

Without her realising it, the crowd had dispersed somewhat and Caleb led Maggie out to the terrace. The balmy air drifted around them on a light scented breeze and she breathed in deeply. There was a secluded gazebo at one end and Caleb took her hand, bringing her over.

'What…what are we doing here?'

Under the trellis roof that had flowers hanging down in a mass of twisting vines and leaves, he turned her to face him. 'Something I've been wanting to do all evening.' He dipped his head to her ear, making a delicious shiver skate up and down her spine. 'Your back has been driving me crazy.'

He pulled her even closer and she gasped when she felt the hardness of his arousal pressing into her belly. It called to her, made her damp with anticipation. She was breathless, waiting for the kiss, the embrace which was inevitable. His mouth hovered infuriatingly over her neck, lips barely skimming her skin. She wound her hands up and around his neck, craving an even closer embrace. Not thinking, not capable, just feeling.

Then his hands were on her bare back and a tremor shot through her. And in that moment his mouth covered hers and she was lost. He traced the outline of her lips, before his tongue delved in and met hers in an intoxicating dance. She was helpless but to succumb, matching his thrusts with her own, shyly allowing him to teach her, guide her.

His hands moulded, traced her waist, her spine, the smooth silky skin. Then one hand moved down and down until it rested just over the material of the dress that lay over her buttocks. She drew back, eyes dark and wide. Breath coming in short gasps. Watching her as he did, his hand went under the material, down until he felt the curve of her bottom, sheathed in silk panties. Her hands tightened on his shoulders.

His eyes were on her flushed face; they glittered with intent as he bent his head and took her mouth again with passionate bruising force, just as his hand went beneath the silk and caressed, smoothed, explored the voluptuous curves. Then his hand dipped all the way down, fingers seeking, underneath, all the way until…

Maggie gasped against his lips as his fingers found the moist evidence of her desire. Stroking back and forth, seeking the most sensitive part. When she would have pulled away, he held her to him fast and it was the most exquisite torture. She couldn't do anything, couldn't move. He was relentless. And then he was there…at that part… A spasm passed through her in response and still she was held captive. Unable to escape a pleasure that was almost too much. Too intense.

With his head bent, pressing fiery kisses against her neck, her head fell back. One hand held her like a vise against his body and with his other hand he was fast bringing her whole body upwards on a spiral of some devilish, overwhelming sensation, the like of which she'd never experienced. She could feel the subtle rhythm of his hard body as it pressed against her, she knew she'd widened her legs to tacitly give him access and their movements became more and more urgent, she didn't know what she was seeking, it was something that lay tantalisingly just out of reach and then… suddenly something gripped her that was so devastating…she stopped breathing for a minute.

Slow seconds later, as if she'd been transported to some other place, she slowly returned and felt her whole being throbbing, pulsating in the aftermath of what felt like an earthquake on her senses. As reality trickled back into her fuzzy mind, as Caleb straightened and loosened his hold slightly, she knew with astounding clarity that she'd just had her first orgasm. She looked up at Caleb, knew that she must have a dazed expression on her face and couldn't even begin to disguise it. She had lost her virginity to her one boyfriend in college, but he'd never ever made her feel anything beyond mild discomfort. This…this, however, was in another league. She heard the murmur of low voices nearby, a tinkle of laughter coming from the ballroom just yards away.

She had come apart in his arms, on little more than the strength of a kiss, had allowed him full access without so much as a murmur of dissent. Without thinking, she just reacted, had to get away. 'Excuse me…I need to go to the bathroom.'

Caleb let her go and she went, hoping she didn't look as devastated by what had just happened as she felt.

He watched her go, sitting back on the seat behind him in a sprawl. His own heart rate was just beginning to return to normal and the unsatisfied ache was acute.

He shook his head grimly; he'd only planned on kissing her. Hadn't planned on the sudden need to maul her sense-less. What was wrong with him? The last time he'd caressed a woman so comprehensively in a public place was when he'd been a gauche teenager. And it had been a girl, not a woman. He cursed himself; he wouldn't be surprised if she had a love bite on her neck.

But she had been so responsive… That subtle touch of feigned innocence was fast pushing him over the edge whenever he came near her. With just his hands on her back! He could still feel the tremor that had run through her, pushing her breasts against him, igniting a fire in his belly…in his loins. And that had intoxicated him beyond the point of reason. She'd been the same that night in London, which he remembered all too well…and yet she'd stopped just when…just when he'd been able to stop. Maybe she was doing it again? Giving him a taste of nirvana, only to bring him to his knees, expose him.

She would not do that to him again. No way. And this time he wouldn't stop. He knew her response wasn't fake. He was arrogantly sure of that. She wouldn't be able to stop herself this time. With a determined lithe push to stand, he was hidden in the shadows for a moment before going in search of Maggie. It was time to claim his prize.

Back in the hotel room, Maggie heard the door click ominously shut behind Caleb. She felt skittish and on edge. She wasn't ready for this. She needed time to process what had happened, had to be in control of her emotions when she gave herself to him. She was still stunned, shocked by the depth of her response to him in the gazebo. As soon as she'd emerged back into the ballroom she'd caught his eye immediately. She'd stood there, fighting the urge to run in the opposite direction as he'd strode towards her, the people melting away either side of him. Without saying a word, he'd halted in front of her, taken her hand and led her out. Not one word. To anyone. And now here they were, back in the hotel. The huge bed just there, in her field of vision.

Maggie turned to face him, not even knowing what to say, but before she could speak, unaware of the turmoil of her thoughts, he went towards the bathroom, shedding his jacket as he did so.

'I'm going to have a shower…'

'Okay…' Panic gripped her voice, making it sound shrill to her ears. 'I'll have one after you.'

He turned at the door, raising one black brow. 'Unless you want to share?'

'No…' she said hastily—too hastily. 'I'll wait.'

He shrugged.

Maggie went out to the balcony and paced up and down with arms wrapped around her body. She couldn't even think coherently. This was happening too fast—way too fast. She was still in pieces after little more than a bout of heavy petting. How would she cope when Caleb…took her completely? Her belly flooded with liquid fire just at the thought and she sat on a chair weakly. She wasn't the woman of the world that he was used to. She was just plain, simple Maggie Holland. The girl with the red hair and freckles who bruised easily and still had scars from falling off trees when she was small. And other scars that he could never know about. She needed time, space. To fight off the inevitable for just a little longer.

The bathroom door opened. She sprang up. He was finished already? Caleb emerged with an indecently small towel around his waist. Hair wet, sleek against his head. Maggie's stricken gaze couldn't escape the wide, broad, muscled chest, a light sprinkling of hair that tapered down to his lean waist. Her eyes skipped over the towel and down over long, long, strong, shapely legs. She gulped. He was shameless under her gaze and indicated the door. 'Bathroom's all yours… Don't be long, Maggie.'

Once inside, she sagged against the door. The mist enveloped her—the heat of his body, the musky scent still in the air. It brought her whole body back into tingling awareness. She had to do something. She couldn't face her ultimate capitulation tonight. Tomorrow, maybe…but not now, not after that…explosive experience.

She kicked off her shoes and went to the mirror, looking at her reflection. Two bright spots of colour highlighted her cheeks; her eyes were too wide and bright. She ran the bath in a desperate attempt to buy some more time to think.

Finally. After waiting for as long as she thought she could, Maggie cautiously opened the bathroom door. Caleb lay on the bed against the pillows with his eyes closed. She emerged slowly. Maybe he was asleep? His eyes snapped open. No such luck. He came up on one arm, a frown appearing when he noticed that she hadn't changed out of the dress. Then a gleam of appreciation lit them.

'Good. I was just fantasising about taking it off you. Come here.'

He thought she'd left it on, on purpose…

Little did he know the terror in her chest—how could he not see it? She moved forward one foot and stopped.

He frowned again. She looked too serious. 'Maggie…' he said warningly.

'Caleb. Wait.' She put up a hand and prayed for courage. 'I'm not going to sleep with you until I've signed the contract.'

He sprang from the bed and Maggie fled back into the bathroom, slamming the door and locking it just as she heard

Caleb's fist make a connection. Her heart hammered against her ribs. The door knob jiggled. She jumped back.

'Maggie… Open up or, so help me God, I will break this door down.'

Desperation made her voice weak. 'You said I'd sign a contract guaranteeing that the house would go back into my mother's name. I want to do that before anything…happens between us.'

'It's already happened, sweetheart.'

She burned on the other side of the door. But at least he wasn't threatening to break it down any more, although he did sound as though he wanted to throttle her.

'Maggie, come out…'

'No way.'

She could hear a muffled oath.

'Not unless you promise not to touch me.'

There was a very long silence. So long that Maggie was afraid he'd left without telling her and now she'd be stuck in the bathroom all night. Then she heard a very low, 'Fine.'

She turned the lock and opened the door. She was relieved when she saw Caleb on the other side of the room in his trousers, arms folded across his chest. His face like thunder. She quivered inwardly but strove for confidence on the outside.

'Do you want to tell me what this is all about?' he asked tightly.

'I want to sign that contract. Once I know for sure you're going to keep your word, then you can…have…make me yours.' Those words alone sent a spiral of heat through her body.

He came a little closer. She backed away slightly. 'If I remember correctly, I made no such assurance; the agreement was that you would move in, become my mistress and then…I would sign the house back to your mother.'

Damn him, he was right. Her shoulders sagged. For a moment Caleb felt something move through him…almost concern. She looked unbelievably vulnerable.

The only thing stopping him from doing what he wanted, going over and shaking her, then kissing her thoroughly was the knowledge that he wanted to do it so badly it scared him. And he would control himself around her, although the gazebo and the passion she had incited still held him in its grip.

Remembering something, he looked and, sure enough, he could see a faint red mark on her neck. It firmed his resolve not to let her see how close he was to losing it. He, Caleb Cameron, one of the wealthiest tycoons in the world, his expertise worth millions, had given a grown woman a love bite. So he stood back. Maybe he needed some time, a little space to make sure he was in control the next time.

Maggie lifted her head and looked at him, those huge green eyes pinning him to the spot.

'Look. You have me. I'm not going to deny you what you want…'

'You want me too, Maggie…'

More than anything.

Her eyes flared for a second, telling him of her agreement even though she didn't say it. 'My dignity and self-respect are pretty much in the gutter right now. All I'm asking is that when we get back you let me sign the contract and then… then…'

There would be no more excuses to avoid the inevitable…

'Okay.'

Maggie thought she hadn't heard him correctly it was so quick. 'Okay?'

'Yes. Fine.' He walked past her, his face expressionless, and started to dress again.

'What…where are you going?'

'Well, Maggie, as you're not willing to share my bed yet…I'm going to go out. You'd better hope to be asleep by the time I return.'

And with that he was gone. Maggie had got what she wanted, so why didn't she feel happy? Why did she want to run out of the door after him and say, Stop! I'm sorry, please come back, take me to bed? She cursed herself, she was only prolonging the pain, the anticipation, the misery. What had she done? Her brain was scrambled beyond all comprehension with him around. But the minute he was gone it was clear again. She had pushed him too far. And now he was gone, back to the function. It was the only place. Or maybe he'd go to a small smoky bar, seek out a kindred soul.

She sat down on a chair. He could have his pick of any number of the beauties who had been vying for his attention the past two evenings. Any number of the beauties in this place. He had gone, to take his pick. He was letting her know that she wouldn't hold him back. But even with that knowledge, her weak body burned for his, ached for a deeper fulfilment than she'd experienced earlier. She changed, washed and climbed into bed, letting sleep obliterate her tortured imaginings.

The next morning Maggie woke and felt safe and secure. A cocoon of warmth surrounded her. She moved experimentally to try and keep it, deepen it, and then froze as she realised where she was. She was comprehensively tucked into the warm embrace of Caleb's arms. Their bodies touched from head to toe. His chest against her back, his long legs spooning hers effortlessly, one almost thrown over her thigh. And he was completely naked. She realized that with burning alarm.

An Important Message from the Editors

Dear Reader,

If you'd enjoy reading romance novels with larger print that's easier on your eyes, let us send you **TWO FREE HARLEQUIN PRESENTS® NOVELS** in our **LARGER PRINT EDITION**. These books are complete and unabridged, but the type is bigger to make it easier to read. Look inside for an actual size sample.

By the way, you'll also get **two surprise gifts** with your **two free books!**

Pam Powers

LP-HP-07

84

she'd thought she was fine. It took Daniel's words and Brooke's question to make her realize she was far from a full recovery.

She'd made a start with her sister's help and she intended to go forward now. Sarah felt as if she'd been living in a darkened room and some- one had suddenly opened a door, letting in the fresh air and sunshine. She could feel its warmth slowly seeping into the coldest part of her. The feeling was liberating. She realized it was only a small step and she had a long way to go, but she was ready to face life again with Serena and her family behind her.

All too soon, they were saying goodbye and Sarah experienced a moment of sadness for all the years she and Serena had missed. But they had each other now, and that's what...

She held...

Like what you see?
Then send for TWO FREE larger print books!

YOURS FREE!

You'll get two great mystery gifts with your two free larger print books.

Yes! I have placed my Editor's **"Free Gifts" seal** in the space provided at right. Please send me 2 free Harlequin Presents® larger print books and my 2 free mystery gifts. I understand I am under no obligation to purchase any books, as explained on the back of this card.

176 HDL ELUE   376 HDL ELZE

FIRST NAME	LAST NAME

ADDRESS

APT.#	CITY

Thank You!

STATE/PROV.   ZIP/POSTAL CODE

Are you a current Harlequin Presents® subscriber and want to receive the larger print edition?
Call 1-800-221-5011 today!

◄ DETACH AND MAIL CARD TODAY

LP-HP-07

The Harlequin Reader Service® — Here's How it Works:

Accepting your 2 free Harlequin Presents® larger print books and 2 free gifts places you under no obligation to buy anything. You may keep the books and gifts and return the shipping statement marked "cancel". If you do not cancel, about a month later we'll send you 6 additional Harlequin Presents® larger print books and bill you just $4.05 each in the U.S. or $4.72 each in Canada, plus 25¢ shipping & handling per book and applicable taxes if any.* That's the complete price and – compared to cover prices of $4.75 each in the U.S. and $5.75 each in Canada – it's quite a bargain! You may cancel at any time, but if you choose to continue, every month we'll send you 6 more books, which you may either purchase at the discount price or return to us and cancel your subscription.

*Terms and prices subject to change without notice. Sales tax applicable in N.Y. Canadian residents will be charged applicable provincial taxes and GST. Offer limited to one per household. All orders subject to approval. Books received may vary. Credit or debit balances in a customer's account(s) may be offset by any other outstanding balance owed by or to the customer. Please allow 4 to 6 weeks for delivery.

Arms held her an easy captive, one hand spread over her breasts, which she could feel coming to life, becoming engorged with rushing blood, her nipples becoming hard, pushing against the warm skin of his hand. If he was to move, just even slightly, curl that hand… She swallowed. Torture. She tried to move but his arms were like steel bands and, when she made a bigger movement, they tightened.

A sleep-rough voice growled in her ear, 'Going somewhere?'

She froze. Again.

'Too late for that. I know you're awake.'

And so was her body. Spectacularly. Betraying her with its eager response to his proximity.

The hand at her breast left and made lazy progress down to her belly, feeling the soft swell under the satin of her negligée, then back up. Maggie's breath came quicker as his hand hovered over the full mounds, the lace of her top chafing unbearably, and then let out a ragged sigh and closed her eyes tightly as it cupped, moulded and caught one taut peak, thumb and forefinger pinching gently, making it even harder until it was like a knife-edge of sensation running all the way down her body to between her legs.

And then, while his hand was busy stimulating one eroge-nous zone, she became aware of how her negligée had ridden up. He was sliding a hair-roughened thigh between her legs, opening her up, nudging past her resistance, and then she could feel the blatant hardness of his arousal *there*, against her, only a mere breath away from being inside, where she longed for fulfilment. She moved her bottom against him. 'Caleb…'

'What…what is it?' His breath was driving her insane. She wanted…she wanted…

'What do you want? This?'

He moved upwards and she could feel the head of him

nudge against her moistness. Her muscles quivered and contracted in anticipation. This was going so fast but, in the heady half sleep limbo land, it was all Maggie could do not to turn and give herself completely.

'Yes…oh, yes.' She bit her lip in an effort not to plead any more.

And then, in a moment so quick and brutal she didn't know which way was up, Caleb was out of the bed and standing there with a towel slung around his waist, hiding the extent of his erection, though she could still feel the size of it, imagine the length of it. His face was stamped with the lines that told her how hard it had been for him to stop. Waves of censure reached out to envelop her.

Confusion showed on her face. Her voice breathless, she said, 'What's wrong?'

'Nothing, Maggie, that a signed contract won't solve.'

He came down and rested on his hands over her, taking in her flushed face, dilated pupils, her still aroused body. 'When we come together it'll be like this, Maggie, so I can watch your face as you give yourself to me.'

So much for her grand announcements last night. Within moments she'd been ready to forget everything—her precious vulnerability swept aside by the burning ache that still pounded in her blood.

She shrank back against the pillows, more humiliated than she had been even that night in London. For at least that time she hadn't tasted the total bliss he could evoke. They hadn't gone so far that she couldn't stop herself. But…he, she remembered uncomfortably, had been in a similar state to now. This time, however, *he* was the one calling a halt. Demonstrating her lack of control over him.

He was binding a silken thread around her, so tight that she knew she'd never be free of it. Even after he was finished with her. Pain made her lash out, her words clumsily inarticulate. 'Wasn't whoever's bed you warmed last night not enough?'

He stopped in the act of straightening up from the bed, his body lithe and supple and heart-stoppingly beautiful. The thought of him with another woman was making her insides fizz with anger. Along with the ache that permeated every bone, betraying how much she wanted him.

He looked at her coldly. 'I, unlike you, have a moral code. I don't share myself around. Aren't you lucky, Maggie?' He gave a short, mirthless laugh. 'I'm all yours. For now. And I won't be made to wait again or, trust me, the agreement will be revoked and I will take a new mistress.'

A rush of elation surged through her—so he hadn't slept with another woman. She was heedless to the incongruity of how happy that made her feel—despite the evidence of their shaky truce in tatters around them, despite the ache, the humiliation, Maggie was suddenly absurdly happy. He flicked her a dismissive glance before turning away. 'We leave for Dublin in an hour.'

CHAPTER SEVEN

JOHN, Caleb's driver, was waiting with the car at the small private airport. Maggie was glad of the distraction of having someone else to talk to as Caleb stood outside the car taking a phone call for a few minutes. In the course of their conversation, Maggie discovered that John had lost his entire family in a tragic accident some ten years previously. He had been working for someone else in the company, but when Caleb had heard the news he'd made John his own driver and now brought him everywhere.

'To tell the truth, love, I don't know what I would have done. He kept me going and there were times…' He stopped and his eyes grew moist. Maggie stretched a hand out to his shoulder in sympathy.

'Sorry, love, it's still…' He recovered and cast a glance out of the car. 'He's a good man. He'll look after you. Loyal to a fault, I'd say. Far too easy on some of them that's tried to put one over on him…'

Caleb slipped back into the car at that moment and John winked at Maggie, lightening the atmosphere, before turning around to drive them into town. She went over his words. Well, Caleb certainly had a fan there. She couldn't fault his behaviour with the man. But she didn't want to know nice things about him; she wanted pettishly for everyone to hate him, to confirm that he was cynical and ruthless.

His voice broke into her thoughts. 'John, drop me off at the office—I have some meetings lined up for the afternoon— then bring Maggie home.'

In the car outside his offices, he turned to Maggie. 'I'll be back about seven and I'll bring the contract. So why don't you burn some water and we can celebrate later?'

Maggie flushed under his pointed gaze that wouldn't let her escape, knowing John could hear their conversation. 'Fine.'

When he was gone, she sat back and breathed properly for the first time that day. Her mind and stomach churned. At least she had a few hours to get control of herself. When they pulled up outside the apartment building, Maggie took her bag from John and watched as he drove away with a cheery wave.

She took a spin out to see her mother that afternoon, to confirm for herself that she was all right. She was so ecstatic and happy and relaxed that Maggie felt real relief for the first time. She was almost a changed woman; she even looked different from the last time Maggie had seen her. Younger. This was her proof, her motivation. She *was* doing the right thing. She knew it. She was heartened for the first time in days as she drove back into town.

Back in the apartment, she decided she couldn't be bothered lying about her ability to cook and made a wild mushroom risotto. Cooking always relaxed her and she needed all the help she could get. Having reluctantly skipped over an old pair of comfy jeans and plain shirt, she figured she'd better dress as he'd expect. So she stood now in the kitchen and felt ridiculously uncomfortable in a silk shirt and light tweed trousers. Her hair, despite her having tried to tame it back into a tidy bun, was already tousled at the nape of her neck. When Caleb walked in, the carpet muffling his entrance, that was what he saw.

Maggie was stirring something in a pot, bending low to smell, a small frown on her face. Then she straightened and started chopping spring onions for a salad. The dexterity with which she chopped told him, as a keen cook himself, that she was no novice. He ignored the strange ache in his chest just from looking at her.

'The burnt water smells surprisingly appetising,' he drawled dryly.

She jumped and whirled around. But quickly regained her composure. He could see that there was tension in the lines of her body that hadn't been there seconds before and bizarrely hated the fact that he had done that.

'Yes…well, I didn't want to give you the satisfaction of thinking you had a live-in cook as well as a mistress. But, as it happens, I can cook quite well.'

'Good. Because I'm starving. I'll have a shower and join you.'

Maggie shrugged negligently, as if she didn't care, but since he'd surprised her at the door her pulse had been thumping out of control.

When he'd gone she ran her wrists under the cold tap to try and calm her pulse. She lifted her hands to her hot cheeks. She was a wreck. Images, fantasies, erotic pictures were taking control of every corner of her brain. She was a walking hormone. She set out the cutlery and a bottle of wine because she knew he'd expect it, but vowed only to have a little herself so that she was in complete control.

And then he was there. He'd dressed down as she would have preferred to, in faded jeans and a T-shirt that was taut across his muscled chest. Wet hair curling just above the collar. His potency, the raw sexuality, reached across the room and called to her, made her want to walk over, sink into him.

'What can I do?'

She shut her eyes for a split second at the lurid images that jumped into her mind's eye at his question. Her voice, when it came, was husky. 'You could bring the salad through; everything else is here.'

Her appetite had just disappeared.

He brought it in and they sat down. Caleb poured them both a glass of wine and lifted his glass high. 'To tonight.'

Maggie blanched and took a deep breath. She just nodded in response. And took a big gulp of wine. So much for her good intentions.

He took a mouthful of the risotto and a look of disbelief came over his face. 'Maggie, this is really good. Where did you learn to do this? Do you know how hard it is to get this right?'

She blushed with acute pleasure and couldn't stop a grin. 'Really?'

'Really. I've eaten in some of the best restaurants in Italy and they certainly haven't done risotto as well as this.'

With pleasure fizzing through her at his rare approval, she explained, 'I worked as a chef's assistant when I was working my way through college. In return for portraits of his family, he gave me extra lessons.'

'Worked your way through college?' Those eyes were narrowed speculatively on hers. She thought quickly. Tom had had millions. Money shouldn't have been an object. Maggie had always refused it, though, seeing it as tantamount to blood money, despite her mother's pleas to let him help her.

She shrugged lightly. 'I thought I wanted to prove to Tom that I could do it on my own, but I soon got bored…' The next words killed her when she thought of the awful bedsit she'd lived in, cockroaches everywhere. 'But of course I didn't last long. Why take the hard way?'

'Why, indeed?' Caleb seemed happy to let it drop. As if she'd jumped out of the box he had her in, but was now safely back inside. They both took another sip of wine.

She had to try and keep him off personal subjects. She was too inclined to speak quickly and openly. He was far too easy to talk to. Like the lunch they'd had in Monte Carlo, they slipped into a light conversation, skating across several subjects. When Caleb poured the last of the wine into her glass she wondered how they'd drunk the whole bottle. She could feel the mellow aftermath through her bones and wanted to wake up. Stay alert.

'I'll make some coffee.' She went to get up and Caleb stayed her with a hand.

'No. You made dinner; I'll do the coffee. Sit on the couch and I'll bring it in.'

His easy courtesy unsettled her. She watched as he proceeded to clear the table and then she heard him moving around the kitchen. She did as he'd said and sat on the couch. That was when she saw it on the table, low down near her feet. The contract. That sobered her up more quickly than any coffee could. She picked it up warily and flicked through it. There, in stark black and white, were the hideous words…

Margaret Holland…become the mistress of Caleb Cameron for two months only…from this date…and the house in question at the following address…revert to the name of Fidelma Holland…but only when said relations have…

Nausea rose. Now that it was in front of her in black and white, she couldn't actually believe that he'd had the gall to draw this up…with the advice of a solicitor? With witnesses? And there were the lines for their signatures. As bold and impersonal and dry as the way her mouth felt right now. Even if she was the one that had begged for their house…had created this situation…this was too much.

He came into the room and Maggie carefully placed it back on the table. He followed her movements as he put down the coffee cups. She picked hers up and placed chilled hands around it, feeling a shudder go through her system.

'So you've seen it.' His voice came low and implacable from her right.

'Yes. Which is, no doubt, what you expected when you directed me over here.'

She could feel him tense beside her. 'I didn't, actually. I'd forgotten I'd put it down. But what's the problem, Maggie? Isn't this what you wanted?'

She put down the coffee jerkily and sprang up away from the couch, willing herself desperately not to cry. 'No! It's not what I wanted. I never wanted any of this. None of it. And certainly not for my private details to be pored over by complete strangers.'

He stood too. She spun away, oblivious to the spectacular backdrop of the city lights starting to come on outside. He came and whirled her round to face him.

'I'm sorry, Maggie, but this is a direct result of your actions. Six months ago you played with fire and now you're getting burnt.'

She was burning up all right.

He captured her close, two harsh hands on her arms. 'You want me, Maggie, as much as I want you. Can you deny it?'

Miserable, intoxicated by his closeness, the contract fading into the background, she couldn't move. He shifted subtly so that she was pressed tight up against the length of him. He brought his hands down her arms and then her two hands were captured behind her back with one of his.

'You want me, don't you?' With his other hand he brushed back a tendril of hair from her face, then threaded through it to cradle her head. She had to fight against wanting to let it sink, fall into his hand. Her body flamed into life everywhere it connected with his...but she wanted to make sure he knew she was fighting it all the way. Had to. It was her only defence.

After seeing that contract, she had a bare thread of dignity left and this was it.

'Yes...' The word was wrung harshly from her. 'I may want you on the outside, but know that on the inside I'm hating you with every breath I take.'

A tension and stillness came into his body. A savage look passed over his face so quickly she might have imagined it. Then his look narrowed and, with his eyes so intensely blue on hers that it hurt, he said, 'Then it's just as well it's not your heart I'm after. Just your body. It's time to finish what you started that night, Maggie.'

His cruelly stark words seared her alive. An ache closed the back of her throat as he bent and took her mouth in a possessive, punishing kiss. And while her foolish, weak body rejoiced in the contact, her heart made a lie of her words— every beat telling her what she didn't want to know, what she didn't want to face up to. What she couldn't face up to yet. His mouth finally gentled and he freed her hands at last, where she hesitated for one weak, desperate moment before giving in under his sensual onslaught and the inevitability of her situation, which meant she couldn't walk away again. She had no choice. She was on a course that was destined to come to its conclusion. A course that she had put them on. A course Tom had put them on six months ago.

As much as they conversely wanted to punch against him for making her feel like this, those treacherous hands climbed up over his chest, up again…until they were around his neck, fingers tangling in the silky strands of hair that brushed his T-shirt. Knowing that somewhere within her all was lost, she gave into what she had for now. And what she had was him— kissing her, making love to her. She pressed close, as close as she could, and wound her arms even tighter round his neck, her kisses matching his, passion for passion. This was all she'd have. His contempt and his passion. So she'd take it.

Caleb pulled back for a moment; he could feel Maggie trembling violently in his arms, had felt something run through her. 'Hey…slow down.' He felt as though he should be comforting her. The light of something very guarded in her eyes caught him and held him; she reminded him of a cornered animal, fighting to protect itself. But that was crazy…

'I'm sorry, I just…I…'

With a finger to her lips, he silenced her. If he didn't know better he'd say she was overwhelmed, inexperienced…but then dismissed that notion. An act. It *had* to be. For some reason it was vitally important.

Her uneven breaths were pushing her breasts against him. He trailed one finger down her heated cheek, around the delicate line of her jaw and down, over her collar-bone, to where the first button held her shirt together. Not allowing her to pull away, he flipped it open, then the next, then the next. He could feel her breath growing more ragged but at least that awful desperation seemed to have gone. That enigmatic light in her eyes had now been replaced by something much more recognisable. Desire.

The shirt fell open to reveal a simple plain sheer bra. He could see the pink aureoles of her nipples, beading, puckering around the tight tips. He brought up his hand and traced the line of her breast, staying away from the sensitive centre, down into the valley, over the mound that spilled from the top, and then finally, slowly, down to where the nipples had grown even harder, tighter.

Maggie was biting into her bottom lip, a shudder running through her, a faint sign of perspiration on her brow as one thumb rotated around that aureole, before finally coming to the centre of where all of her nerve-endings were screaming for release. With a thumb and forefinger, he pinched gently and Maggie felt her legs buckle. Caleb caught her and, just feet away from them, brought her over and lowered her on to the couch. Her response was testing his control to the limit. She lay back and watched as he pulled his T-shirt impatiently over his head, revealing his perfect torso.

He put his hands over hers at her sides and pressed a quick kiss to her mouth, before moving down, lips over her neck, the thumping pulse and down, into the valley, before closing in a kiss over one aching peak. Her arms held captive, Maggie writhed with the pleasure as his mouth moved to the other side and the onslaught started all over again. She couldn't think, couldn't speak. All she was blissfully aware of was the heaven of sensations Caleb was taking her to as his mouth sucked, teeth nipped.

With a graceful movement he pulled her up and pushed the shirt from her shoulders, unhooked her bra and pulled it off. He set her back and looked his fill.

'So beautiful.'

He traced the curves of her waist, her soft belly, and his fingers halted at the button on her trousers. He pressed her back down and came over her, his chest rubbing deliciously against her breasts. His mouth covered hers, her arms wound around his neck and their tongues met in a dance that took her breath away. The hand at her trousers undid the button. She felt constricted and wanted them off, lifting her hips to help him pull them down, kicking them free, their lips still clinging together.

He stopped and looked down, saw her plain white knickers, her slender, shapely legs. He ran a hand upwards over one silken flank and hovered close to where he wanted nothing more than to feel the evidence of her desire. He heard, felt her breath stop.

She was so beguiling, in nothing but the knickers, her whole body covered in a dusting of freckles, and he wanted her more desperately than he'd ever wanted anyone. His jeans contained his arousal…just.

In the next instant he lifted her into his arms and brought her into the bedroom. She felt curiously vulnerable to him, naked in his arms against his chest, her arms tight around his neck. Maggie marvelled dimly that she had thought that when they got to this stage she'd be paralysed with nerves…but there was a fever in her blood that drowned out anything other than Caleb…and her. It felt right. And good. As if how they had got here didn't matter—what mattered was that they were here.

Once in the bedroom, he put her down on unsteady feet. Her eyes were dark and fathomless. He reached around and undid the pins holding her hair back and it fell in a curtain of waves and curls around her shoulders and down her back. Without taking his eyes off hers, he undid his jeans and pulled them down, stepping out of them.

He was naked. Maggie's hot gaze moved down and took him in. He was magnificent. Having been with only one man before, she felt out of her depth…and yet, conversely…*knew* what to do. It was something she couldn't even begin to figure—it was just an innate knowing. Something between *her* and this man. A knowing that made every cell in her body ache to have him inside her, filling her. She shook with the force of the emotion running through her and yet, to her surprise, it didn't scare her.

She looked up for a brief moment and the expression in Caleb's eyes set her pulse on fire. Filled with a sense of sensual adventure, emboldened by his dark look, his obvious arousal for her, she reached out, dimly wondering how on earth she had the nerve, and closed one small hand around the length of him. She could feel it pulse, jump slightly, the satin smooth skin moving against the hard shaft. Her hand looked tiny and pale around it, barely able to encircle it. She felt a liquid coil of desire within her.

She looked up into Caleb's face and his eyes were slits; there were slashes of dark colour on each cheek bone and he struggled with his breath. The thought that she was doing this to him made her feel exultant in her sexuality.

He was gone beyond the place of reason or coherence. The intoxicating mix of her wide-eyed innocence and her obvious know-how was too much. He shook with the need to be inside her, filling her…this woman, no one else. He wouldn't, couldn't think of all the other men she'd done this for. It would kill him. He vowed to take her so completely that she'd never want another man again. He stopped her hand with his, his voice was guttural, hoarse. 'Maggie…stop unless you want this to be over very quickly.'

He moved her back to the bed, tumbling her down. She watched as he came over her on two strong arms. She moved back to allow him room and then he was running his hands down, over the peaks and hollows, lingering, sometimes tracing with his mouth where his hands had been and then his mouth hovered over her belly button, his tongue flicking out to taste.

His hands reached her knickers and slowly but surely started to pull them down. They dropped on to the floor. Now she was bared completely and she felt Caleb nudge her legs open with his body. She felt a breath *there*, where the molten core of her was. She couldn't look and flung an arm over her face in a fit of shyness. His hands came under her buttocks, tilting her slightly, and then she felt his tongue exploring, leaving a wet, hot trail as it crept up one inner thigh, then the other, before spreading her even further, opening her up so that his mouth…and tongue could seek and find that rock-hard small piece of flesh that no other man had ever touched with such intimacy.

When his tongue found it, circled it, sucked…she thought she'd die…and then his tongue moved down…and entered her. She tensed and arched her back. Her other hand gripped the sheets. Her breathing was so fractured and tortured she thought she might pass out. How could he do this…make her feel like this…so liquid and wanton and…? She couldn't stop herself—the spiral was building, like a coil tightening; his tongue was harder, thrusting deeper, until finally she was pushed to the point of no return and she came, her whole body bucking in the aftershock. Her arm was still over her face; she was too mortified to look and felt tears under her eyelids at the intensity of emotion she was feeling. She could feel Caleb move up over her sensitive body and he brought her arm down. She blinked away the tears before he could see them.

He kissed her so deeply that she could taste herself on him. He was drunk on the scent of her, the taste of her, the feel of her and couldn't wait any longer. After slipping on protection, he fought the urge to thrust in so deep and far that he'd have immediate relief. She was looking at him now, an intense look of concentration on her face which made him feel a fierce tenderness, but he was in the grip of something so powerful that he couldn't dwell on it…or question it.

'Don't close your eyes, Maggie.'

She shook her head. She couldn't look away even if she wanted to. She felt him push against her slick folds and lifted her hips to him. He brought a hand under her back, arching her to him, and pushed in further. And further. Her eyes opened wide at the exquisite sensation. He was so big…but she could feel her muscles taking him in, and then he thrust again. The entire hard length of him was within her tight embrace. She still had that look of concentration on her face, as though it was all she wanted to do—give him this pleasure. The force of how it made him feel rippled through his body.

Her legs instinctively came around his buttocks, her hands on his shoulders as he pulled out before filling her again. Her eyes on his, their gazes locked, with steady thrusts Caleb brought Maggie into another universe. Where she forgot time and space, her name, everything. He waited until her body convulsed around his and then, with beads of sweat on his brow, gave in to his own earth-shattering capitulation.

As he curled his body around Maggie's, Caleb felt for the first time in his life as if he'd finally come home.

What a ridiculous thought…

But, more importantly, finally…she was his.

Maggie took the cup of tea she'd just made and walked over to the huge window in the sitting room. Hardly seeing the view, her thoughts inward, she felt…curiously still…and empty. As if something monumental had shifted within her. She was very much afraid she'd never be the same. And she knew she'd compartmentalised it somehow, put it into some corner where she wouldn't have to deal with it…just yet. Her whole body ached, muscles protesting if she moved too quickly, and when she'd looked in the mirror earlier she'd been shocked at the bruises on her skin. She blushed then as she remembered raking Caleb's back with her nails and wondered if she'd left him with marks too.

She took a sip of tea, feeling the hot liquid go down, warming her insides, which felt curiously cold. Maybe this was just her defence mechanism kicking in. All she *was* willing to acknowledge was that he had made her take leave of her senses and that the two of them had ignited a passion that scared her with its intensity. And it had started a craving ache that she knew wouldn't be sated until she saw Caleb again.

The phone rang, piercing the air, and she jumped. Little fiery shivers of sensation raced along her nerve-endings as she already anticipated his voice on the other end. Images of last night flooded her head. Thank God he couldn't see her.

'Hello?'

'There's a courier on the way around for—'

'Okay, fine.'

'See you later, then.'

'Fine.'

She cut him off. Didn't want him to say it. She knew exactly what he was talking about. Their conversation couldn't have been more sterile. He was talking about the contract. In the headiness of last night, when he'd swept her so effortlessly into that vortex of need and want and pleasure, she'd forgotten all about it. Only to wake this morning to an empty bed and the contract beside her. She smiled grimly—that just about summed up what was going on. He'd signed his part and left a curt note:

Countersign and I'll send over a courier. Consider it done.

So it was done. Her mother had her house back…and, in seven weeks and a bit, Maggie would be free to walk away. Curiously, the thought didn't fill her with the elation she'd thought it would. Was she really so pathetic? She jerked away from the phone and the window and went to rinse out the cup. She found a pen, signed the contract and put it in an envelope Caleb had left behind. Then she waited for the courier down-stairs. She almost thrust it at him when he arrived, more distraught than she would have imagined or thought she'd be.

CHAPTER EIGHT

OVER the following days the packages started to arrive. Velvet boxes that held stunning jewels. Usually with a note, nothing endearing, something curt like: *For tonight* or *This'll go with something black.* Maggie stopped being stunned and saying thank you because Caleb didn't seem to like it. He told her he expected her to wear them…much like she'd wear a designer dress. As if he were just kitting her out. And with each piece, whether it was a bracelet or a necklace or earrings, she felt cheaper and cheaper. More and more humiliated.

As much as she tried, she just found it so hard to put on all those jewels and parade around like some gilded lily. It made her uncomfortable…uneasy. Went against all her moral and political sensibilities. If he were giving them to her from a place of genuine pleasure, *in her*, then that would be different. But that fantasy belonged in a world that didn't exist.

She had to realise, now that she was sharing his bed…this was his usual *modus operandi*. She was no different and she'd be a fool to dream otherwise. On the fifth day, after the fourth night in his bed, when she received a priceless diamond bracelet, it finally drove her from the apartment, the sense of rising panic too much. She walked…for hours, for miles. And eventually ducked into an old cinema in an effort to block out the thoughts that hounded her brain like whirling dervishes.

'Where the hell have you been?'

Maggie tried not to quail at the anger stamped into Caleb's features, but she could feel an old familiar panic rise up.

Caleb is not Tom...

She closed the front door behind her. 'I went to the cinema, Caleb. You can't lock me in here every day—'

'Oh, can't I?' he said threateningly as he advanced on her. The colour leached from her face, stopping him in his tracks. Her eyes were huge. He forced himself to calm down. She was back. She was here. Had he really thought she'd try and leave once the contract was signed? But he had...for a moment.

He thrust a hand through his hair. 'Maggie, look... Of course I can't lock you in here. I got back and you were gone...I don't know, I guess I thought...' He shook his head. 'It doesn't matter. Just call me next time...'

Maggie couldn't believe it, slowly allowing herself to calm again. He actually looked...almost shaken. Had he really thought she'd run away? As if! She had no doubt that if she had even tried anything like that, he'd have reneged on the agreement, contract or no.

'I don't actually have your mobile number,' she said dryly.

'Well, let's remedy that now.' He took her bag with proprietary ease and fished out her phone. She looked on, bemused, as he punched in his number and handed it back.

'You don't need mine?'

He looked addled. 'Yes, I do.'

He handed her his phone and she put in her number and handed it back. Somehow, she felt a twitch at the corner of her mouth. Was it hysteria? Who cared? Suddenly a lightness was bubbling up and she couldn't hold it in. Caleb caught her rapidly contorting face and frowned for a second. 'What—?'

She couldn't stop it; laughter bubbled out and she gasped with the effort to control it. 'I'm sorry…it's…just…a bit…'

'After the fact?' he asked with a twitch on his mouth too. He watched as she tried to control herself, felt her lightness reach out to touch him. She gasped in big breaths and wiped at the tears that had sprung from her eyes. He reached out a finger and trailed it over one cheek, saying almost wonderingly, 'You're even more beautiful when you laugh… You should do it more often.'

Her belly quivered at his touch, then she hiccuped, 'Well, I haven't had much cause lately.'

Or ever…

Something dark crossed Caleb's face and she could see him close up again. No! she wanted to say. Stay with me. He dropped his finger; she felt bereft. She controlled herself again. They were still standing just inside the door.

'I've put on some chicken…how does that sound?'

'You cook?' she asked inanely.

His mouth quirked. 'Apparently quite well.'

She shrugged, trying not to look too impressed, finding herself inordinately relieved to be eating in. They'd eaten out every other night so far, each restaurant more glittering and exclusive than the last, and Maggie was tired. 'The proof will be in the eating,' she quipped quickly, not wanting him to see her relief.

'Ouch.' He winced and started to head back towards the kitchen. 'Not all of us were trained by chefs; some of us had to learn the hard way.'

She followed him into the sparkling, brand new kitchen, curious. 'So where did you learn, then?'

As she watched, he seemed to know what he was doing, tossing a salad with fluid ease. It would be just like the man to be able to do everything perfectly.

'My mother can't cook to save her life, or my father, and in lean times, when Dad became bankrupt and when Mother left to tout for her next rich ticket, I had to cook for them or we'd all have gone hungry.'

Maggie gasped, 'But you were only a child!'

He shrugged negligently. 'Once my mother married again in Brazil, we had a housekeeper, but I still used to cook for Dad in England. I enjoyed it, even if I was one of the only boys doing home economics when I went to school there in my teens.'

She shook her head; something flipped over in her at this more human side to him. 'Wow, that was pretty brave! I remember the ribbing we used to give the boys in our school.'

She thought of his words then and remembered something that Michael Murphy had said that day of the funeral. 'You said your dad became bankrupt…was…is that why you don't go after your enemies with total ruthlessness?'

He looked up, his eyes narrowed sharply on hers. She flushed—what was she doing? They'd been actually getting along.

He wouldn't let her escape, lifting a brow.

'What I mean is…Mr Murphy said something about you not being known for being…so merciless,' she finished lamely.

He stopped what he was doing and leant both hands on the counter top. 'And yet I was merciless to you and your family…?'

She nodded miserably, desperately wishing she hadn't opened her mouth.

'I only fight back when provoked beyond reason…and you and your stepfather did that, Maggie. You can spare me the armchair psychoanalysis.'

He had retreated back behind the cool front. She backed away from the door. 'I'll just have a quick shower.'

He looked at the empty doorway for a long time. For a few moments there, they'd shared a lightness he rarely encountered with anyone. And then, with that one comment…she'd actually pinpointed something that was so fundamental about the way he lived, did business, something that no one else had ever picked up on. Not the broadsheets, tabloids, reporters…and they had done their best over the years to figure out the Cameron phenomenon. The way he'd built his fortune from next to nothing, first in Rio and London, then encompassing the world. All by the age of thirty-six.

The truth was, the way he conducted his business life *was* inextricably bound up with his past experiences. Seeing his father comprehensively ruined, become a shell of a man, only to be deserted by his tempestuous wife as soon as the money was gone, had left deep wounds. Somewhere deep down, he'd vowed that would never happen to him. His hands had curled to fists and he just noticed them now, consciously uncurling them. He willed the dark memories away. Maggie was just trying to push his buttons…and he wouldn't let her.

'What can I do?' Maggie's chin was tilted, her voice almost defiant as she spoke from the doorway. She was determined not to let Caleb see how his shut-down had affected her. His face was still grim. He flicked her a glance, taking in the damp hair that coiled down past her shoulders, a soft V-neck cashmere sweater that clung to her curves. Couldn't help but notice the shadow of something—was it hurt?—that lit her eyes an intense green. Distracted by that and how it made him feel, he listed off abstractedly, 'Set the table, get some cutlery, glasses…'

'Yes, sir,' she muttered under her breath and started

opening cupboards. She would not let him see how hurt she was but it was still there, just under her skin like a wound. What had she expected, after all? She shook her head at herself and stretched up to look for plates.

Suddenly she felt her waist grabbed and she was whirled around and into Caleb's chest so fast that the breath left her body. He brought two hands around her face, caressing her jaw. Immediately she could feel her body responding, sinking, craving… She looked up helplessly.

'Maggie…just…don't try to figure me out. I don't need that. All I need is you…' he looked to her mouth '…this.'

He bent his head and met her lips with his, kissing, drawing in her full bottom lip, tugging and teasing before sliding his tongue in to delve deep and stroke hers. Her arms moved around his waist and clung, hands moving unconsciously over his shirt. She guessed it was an apology of sorts. But he was also saying that he didn't need anything from her, not her opinions, not her thoughts, not her concern…certainly not her heart. And, while he kissed her, she could forget that…but when he stopped, she knew the pain would filter through. So, in an effort to avoid that, she kissed him back, hoping, wishing that he'd never stop. She craved the contact that would obliterate her churning thoughts.

He pulled back. Looking down, he could see Maggie's eyes still closed and her lips full and pouting. He groaned. She opened her eyes. They looked slumberous. She looked down to his mouth.

'Don't stop…' There was something desperate in her voice.

Reaching up on tiptoe, she brought Caleb's head down again; she couldn't reach, she was so much smaller and her mouth hovered inches away, like a succulent fruit. When she said again, 'Please…don't stop,' it lit a flame of desire so strong that he couldn't resist and he lifted her up, sitting her on the island in the kitchen.

Coming between her legs, he cupped her face again, kissing her long and deeply. He could feel her hands resting on his chest, then the fingers move to open the buttons of his shirt, slipping inside to caress his skin. It made a tremor of intense longing surge through him.

He pulled up her sweater, taking it off completely, and her breasts were bare, pert and pink with arousal; he cupped one and ran a thumb over and back over the peak. Her head fell back with the sensation and then he took it into his hot mouth, rolling it, sucking. Maggie was gasping, her hair damp against her back. When he lifted his head finally, she tried to open his shirt the rest of the way but her hands were shaking too much. Caleb's hands took hers away. 'Let me…'

He opened his shirt and Maggie felt the ache growing between her legs. She wriggled on the island and Caleb threw his shirt aside, pulling her against him and running his hands over her back, his mouth on her neck, her shoulder. Her blood was thumping, pumping out of control. She wanted him… now. She wasn't aware that she'd even said the words out loud until she heard, 'Really? You want me here? Now?'

She couldn't believe they were still in the kitchen, that she'd been so bold, that she'd *begged* him to kiss her, take her, but it was too late. And she knew she was blocking out something…some hurt.

Coward.

She nodded jerkily, glad to see that, despite his cool, rational words, he was breathing fast too, his eyes dark and pupils dilated. His hand went to her jeans and she lifted her hips so he could pull them off.

Her eyes followed his hands as they undid his belt and it

snaked through the loops on his trousers just below his taut stomach. She breathed in, her stomach tight with desire, slid off the island and opened the button on his trousers herself, pressing kisses to his chest, finding a nipple, biting gently.

His hand captured her head and she heard a whistle of breath escape through his teeth. 'Maggie, Maggie, what are you doing to me?'

He stilled her hand and picked her up, carrying her into the bedroom. He placed her down on the bed and stripped off his trousers and briefs. Then he pulled her panties down, over her hips and off. Invaded by a wanton, hitherto unexplored need, she instinctively arched her back, her hips rising to meet him as he spread her legs with his thigh. He leant back for a second and, getting protection, rolled it on, then he pressed down, close over her whole body and thrust in, so completely and deeply that she cried out. The spiral of ecstasy finally obliterated all coherent, troubling thoughts. Just as she'd wished and hoped for.

'More wine?'

Maggie shook her head and placed a hand over her glass. She was still finding it hard to meet Caleb's eyes. An hour after dinner had been ready, they were eating.

And all because…all because…

Maggie wished the ground would just open up and let her disappear. *She* had begged him to kiss her, not to stop. *She* had practically ripped his clothes off him. *She* had initiated an act of lovemaking that had combusted around them like a white-hot flame. She'd been half naked in the *kitchen*. An awful mortification twisted her insides.

He'd taken her hard and fast and so totally that she still felt dizzy. And she knew it had been motivated purely by her desire to avoid being faced with his indifference to her feelings—feelings she wasn't ready to acknowledge. That was a route to self-destruction if ever there was one.

'Maggie?'

Reluctantly, she forced herself to meet his gaze.

'Do you want to tell me what's causing that pained expression on your face? Or will I just assume it was my cooking?'

Her gaze slipped away, then back. Of course he'd be used to his mistresses taking the initiative; they'd no doubt be far more experienced than her in the ways of lovemaking to keep a man like Caleb happy. In contrast to her inner agitation, he seemed to think nothing out of the ordinary had just happened. She forced a bland, cool look and smiled. 'Nothing, and your chicken was…delicious.'

It had been sublime, cooked to perfection. And would have been even better had they eaten it when it had been ready. That thought made her cringe inwardly again.

'Flattery?' he mocked with a raised brow. 'Trying to throw me off the scent of something, Maggie?'

She couldn't be that transparent, could she? She could feel a red tide ascending.

'Your blushes make you as easy to read as a book.'

A sudden pain gripped her. Thank God he thought he had her so well sized up that every time she blushed it meant the opposite to what she was really feeling. But the pain struck sharp. She got up to clear away the plates. When she came back in, he grabbed her wrist and pulled her down into his lap.

'What?' Why did she have to sound so breathless? And why was her body coming to vibrant life so easily? Traitor.

'I've got a surprise for you… You didn't spot anything outside when you came back?'

Maggie shook her head. Where was this going?

'I wanted to show you earlier, but then you were so late… and we got distracted.'

He felt Maggie tense against his body. She was such a mass of contradictions. Making love to him with an intensity and passion he'd never encountered, only to spend the next hour avoiding his eyes. He was used to having to firmly extricate himself from cloying embraces after making love and with Maggie…she was the complete opposite, couldn't wait to get away from him. And, for the first time, he actually felt a little…piqued.

But then she was nothing but a heartless, mercenary…he wanted to say *bitch*, but it felt wrong. He couldn't actually say the word, even in his head. In an effort to avoid thinking about it, he stood abruptly, taking Maggie with him. Her serious eyes were focused on his face; he could feel a responding heat unfurl just under her look.

'Come downstairs; I'll show you.'

He took her hand and led her out of the apartment. Down the lift, to the door and out into the rapidly darkening night. They were on the street.

'Well?' he asked a little impatiently after a few minutes' silence.

Maggie looked up and down, more and more bemused. 'Caleb, I don't know what you want me to—' She stopped suddenly and he felt her hand tighten on his. 'My car…my car is gone… It was just here…' She pulled free and stepped closer to the road. 'Where…? I mean, I parked it just here. I know I did.' She could feel panic start to rise and turned to face him. 'Maybe it's been towed. I paid the meter earlier, though; no one could possibly want to take it—'

'Maggie, stop.' Caleb came and turned her back round to face the cars parked on the street. He brought his arms around her body and pointed at a gleaming brand-new Mini Cooper, sitting in exactly the same spot as her car had been.

'No…my one was old, remember?' she said, slightly bitterly in light of his recent opinion on why she might own a car like it.

'I got it towed away, Maggie. It was an accident waiting to happen, believe me. This is your new car.' He dangled a key in front of her face.

What? Just like that?

'But…I… Where…what did you do with mine?'

'It's probably the size of a tin can by now.'

As Maggie was still held in the circle of his arms, her back to him, she couldn't stop the wobble in her lip. She felt inexplicably as though Caleb had just pulled her soul out, wrung it dry and handed it back. She knew it was just a car, but it had been *hers*, the first thing she'd bought. A symbol of her independence from Tom. She'd taught her mother how to drive in it. And now, without so much as a by your leave, Caleb had thrown it away.

She bit down furiously on her lip to stop the tremble. There was no way he could know how much this hurt her—he'd probably think she was just acting again. He was still dangling the key. She picked it out of his hand—still hadn't said anything, couldn't trust herself. He let her go and she walked over. It was so silly, she knew, to be this upset. And she was angry. She blinked her eyes, ignored the ache in her heart, took a deep breath and turned around with a huge smile on her face. 'It's beautiful. Sorry, I was just stunned…I've never…I mean it's been so long since anyone gave me a gift so generous…'

The anger and pain galvanised her actions; she came back and reached up to kiss him and pouted prettily. 'I presume it'll be mine after the two months are up? After all, I do need a car...' here she trailed a finger down his front and the gesture jarred uncomfortably with him '...and the jewels too...?'

She looked up coquettishly from under long lashes and could see the hoped for reaction set in, the hardening of his jaw, that harsh glitter in his eyes. She was acting true to the form he expected. And it made her sick inside. But also, bizarrely, for some reason, protected.

'Of course.' As much as he detested her behaviour, he could feel a sense of relief flood through him. Had he actually for one moment thought that she was anything other than *this*? What a fool! It somehow helped to justify giving her priceless gems, even the car.

It was no less than he'd given any other mistress.

You're just giving into her mercenary little heart. It's what she wanted all along...and more...

He furiously reasoned with himself—her car, if it had been hers, which he seriously doubted, had been a liability...and, as for the jewels...he *wanted* to adorn her luminous skin in fiery rubies and flashing emeralds. It was purely for his pleasure alone. Their collective worth was chicken-feed to him. He took her hand and led her back inside. Maggie shut out the image of the sparkly new car that she would have traded any day of the week to have her own again.

She took the car for a drive the next day, on a visit to her mother. When they came out of the house a few hours later, her mother sounded suspicious.

'He's a very generous employer, giving you a car just like that...'

Maggie tried to avoid the scrutiny of her mother's gaze. 'Yes, well, the other thing was a rattle trap and you were the one always telling me to get rid of it.'

'I know, but I also know how much you loved it.'

'Yes, well…' Maggie said airily. 'As Caleb's assistant now, I have to look a certain way, maintain a certain… image.'

Her mother had that all too familiar worried frown again. 'Maggie…are you sure everything is all right? I remember that you and Caleb had that—'

Maggie cut her off rapidly. 'Mum, that was dinner—once. I'm not in his league—don't worry.'

She leant in to kiss her. She longed to give in and lean on her mother…but years of being the support had ingrained her sense of responsibility too deep.

'And what about your painting?'

Maggie pulled back. 'That'll just have to wait for a few weeks.'

She didn't look convinced but let Maggie sit in the small car before saying innocently, 'I've invited Caleb for lunch next week, to say thank you for being so kind—I'm still so embarrassed that Tom tried his best to ruin him.'

Maggie looked up wildly. Caleb *here*? At the house? With her mother gushing about how wonderful he was?

'He's far too busy. He can't possibly make time—' She went cold. 'Hang on a second, did you say *invited*?'

'Yes, dear. I asked Michael Murphy to call him and extend the invitation; he said yes immediately. You'll come too, of course.'

Her words were still reverberating in Maggie's head as she arrived back at the apartment. Disaster. Her mother was likely to give everything away with just a few words. Yet she knew if she tried to dissuade Caleb from going, he'd suspect something immediately and be even more determined to go. No doubt he was wondering what on earth Tom's widow wanted with him. Maggie would have to watch her mother like a hawk and just make sure she said nothing incriminating. Her head was throbbing.

The phone was ringing as she got in, but stopped before she could reach it. She knew it was Caleb, could feel his impatience as, sure enough, her mobile started to shrill.

'Where were you?'

'Out…I went for a drive; is that okay?'

He grunted.

She had to check, to confirm for herself. 'I believe my mother has asked you for lunch…?'

Please say no, laugh, say you won't be able to go…

'Yes and I'm looking forward to it… I'm even intrigued, you could say. I was calling to say I'll be back at eight.'

Maggie felt sick as the phone went dead.

That night and for the next few days they seemed to settle into an uneasy truce. Uneasy because Maggie had to guard her tongue all the time. Especially when Caleb was relaxed and charming. Which, she hated to admit, was more often than not. Unless something from the past reared its ugly head. Then he shut down. By day she stocked up on some art supplies, explored the outdoor terrace of the apartment, even tried to do a little painting, and by night…by night, she and Caleb entered another realm, where no words were spoken, no words were blessedly needed as he took her to height after height of pleasure.

As the day of the lunch approached, Maggie was hoping against hope that Caleb had forgotten about it, but her wishes were dashed when he emerged from the shower on the Sunday morning.

'What time is lunch?'

He'd remembered.

Maggie sat up in the bed, pulling the sheet up, still absurdly shy in front of Caleb, even though just minutes before he'd wrought a response from her that still had her pulse beating fast. She willed down the tell-tale heat with monumental effort.

'One o'clock.'

As if she didn't already know that his mind was as sharp as a sword. She fled into the bathroom so she wouldn't have to watch him dress and, when she emerged, she could hear him whistling merrily in the kitchen. As if he didn't have a care in the world. She envied him his cool ability to ride roughshod over people's lives and ignored the traitorous tingle in her body and the voice that whispered to her how much she enjoyed *certain* aspects of being with him.

On the way out of the city she asked him to stop by a newsagents so she could get some papers. He looked at her with a strange expression.

'What?'

'Nothing…' He lifted his brows innocently.

'I can read, you know. And I do like to keep up with current affairs. I'm sorry if your usual…' The word stuck in her craw.

'Girlfriends?' he supplied with a quirk on his lips.

'Mistresses…are more intellectually challenged.'

He lifted a hand and ticked off on his fingers. 'Actually, the last one was a human rights lawyer; the one before that was a hedge fund manager; the one before that—'

'Okay, okay, I get the point. So I'm your dumbest mistress—'

He'd parked the car and leant over suddenly, thinking of how dry and sterile and *boring* those women had been. 'Dumb? That's not a word I'd use to describe you, Maggie.' And he was suddenly surprised to know that he really meant it. In the last few days he'd had more stimulating conversations with her than he'd had with anyone in a long time. And he was uncomfortably aware of how much he'd come to look forward to walking in that door every day…as much as he might deny it to himself.

When he looked at her the way he was now, with that heated expression in his eyes, Maggie just wanted to drown in the blue depths. She willed herself back to sanity and felt for the door handle, not even able to break away, much as she wanted to. Finally she found it and practically fell out of the car, fled into the shop…and then came back.

'Sorry, I should have asked, did you want anything?'

Caleb just shook his head and watched her leave. That something was niggling him again. Like a constant barely-there buzzing in his head, he couldn't put his finger on it, it was so elusive. And he had to acknowledge the dark part of him that didn't want to investigate what it was.

By the time they reached the house he'd put it from his mind. Maggie turned around to face him in the car when they pulled in, something urgent in her movements.

'My mother thinks I'm working for you as an assistant, so please don't disabuse her of that, and Caleb…'

He faced her properly, momentarily stunned by the serious expression on her face, the unmistakable protective light in her eyes. He'd seen it before, in Monte Carlo.

'If you do or say *anything* to upset her…the deal will be off—we'll cope somehow, but I will walk away and you can have the house.'

'How on earth could I upset your mother, Maggie?'

'She had nothing to do with anything, Caleb, nothing. Just remember it's me you're punishing, not her.'

And she got out of the car.

For a second Caleb sat there. Punishing her? As he watched her walk to the door, the soft folds of the dress she wore flowing round her hips and legs, as he felt the familiar surge of desire that wasn't abating one tiny bit, the thought that she felt he was punishing her was not a comfortable one. And he didn't know why. Because that was what he'd set out to do all along, wasn't it?

He stepped out, meeting Maggie at the door just as it opened. He almost didn't recognise the woman who stood there. She certainly looked different from how he remembered her—as almost grey, fading into the background. This woman looked…vibrant. Although he could see something in her eyes, some light that had been diminished, and there was a distinct wariness, a jumpiness there. He could see traces of the beauty she'd once been. A different beauty from Maggie's, but there all the same. Maggie was hugging her and re-introducing them, as they'd met in London. He could feel the waves of warning emanate from her tightly held body and suddenly wanted to reassure her. He fought down the urge, telling himself he must be getting soft.

Maggie's mother showed them into the front room, the same one that he'd been in before, where he'd seen Maggie again for the first time since they met in London. When they had drinks in their hands, she sat nervously on the edge of a chair.

'Mr Cameron—'

He smiled urbanely. 'Caleb, please.'

She smiled. 'Very well, Caleb. I just wanted to say…thank you so much for being so generous. I don't know how we can ever repay you. You have no idea how much this house meant, means to us…me and Maggie.' She took Maggie's hand beside her. 'After my beloved Brendan died, it was all I had to remind me of him…'

'Mrs Holland, I had no intention of making you suffer. Once Maggie explained the situation to me, I couldn't have taken your house too…'

'But…I know what this house is worth, Mr Cameron—'

Caleb could see tears come into her eyes. Then, he just *knew*. Maggie had told him the truth. This woman had had nothing to do with Tom's plans.

'Mrs Holland, I'm making full use of Maggie while I'm here in Dublin. When I leave, I'll be more than satisfied to leave the house to you. Believe me, it's enough.'

He looked at Maggie. She was burning up and he could see the pulse thumping erratically against her neck. She finally managed to get out a strangled, 'Mum…shouldn't we check the lunch?'

CHAPTER NINE

BY THE time they were eating their desserts, Maggie was relatively relaxed. Caleb had been charm personified, her mother suitably impressed and Maggie had kept quiet. She had just made coffee and was bringing it on a tray into the dining room.

'And how on earth did you manage to persuade her to get rid of that car? Believe me, I've been trying for years; you would have thought it was like some kind of family pet. The only reason she didn't drive it over to London was because she knew it'd never survive the journey…'

Maggie stood, stunned into immobility by her mother's chatter, and then spoke quickly, putting down the tray, giving out the cups, trying not to slop the coffee everywhere with her shaking hands.

'Mum…I'm sure Mr Cameron doesn't want to hear about my banger. He did me a favour. I grew out of that long ago.'

'But Maggie, only a few weeks ago you told me—'

'More dessert, Mum? More coffee?'

'We haven't drunk it yet, Maggie,' Caleb said dryly, an assessing gleam in his eyes as he took in Maggie's all too obvious discomfiture.

She managed to distract her mother with something else

and prayed that Caleb wouldn't have taken too much notice. A short while later they stood up.

'Mr—I mean, Caleb…' Maggie's mother laughed almost girlishly—the effect of a couple of glasses of wine. Maggie cringed; she was practically flirting with the man. And while she loved nothing more than seeing this more relaxed, peaceful side to her mother, she wished it could have been with anyone else. Not the all too dangerous Caleb, who would be sizing up every word.

'I'll give you the guided tour…'

'Mum, we should really be going.'

Caleb smiled dangerously, confirming her fears. 'Nonsense, Maggie, there's nothing pressing and I'd love to see the house.'

He extended a gallant arm to Mrs Holland, who looked at Maggie triumphantly.

'See? Now, why don't you get started on the washing-up and let me show Caleb around?'

They were gone for what felt like ages. Maggie's brain was working overtime when she thought of her bedroom, which hadn't been redecorated since her teens, with all her teen idol posters still up and the flowery bedspread. With the move to London for college and only intermittent visits since, she hadn't had the time. Or inclination, after returning from London.

Then Caleb walked into her line of vision in the garden. Alone. He stood there with hands in his pockets, surveying the view. Spectacular in a black sweater and dark trousers that hugged every bit of his tall, lean length. She sighed. And jumped when her mother appeared.

'Well, love. Now there's a man.'

I'll say…

She joined Maggie at the sink and started to help dry the

dishes. Caleb disappeared from view and Maggie felt scared suddenly, imagining when he'd be gone for good.

Her mother put an arm around her shoulders and Maggie leant into her, taking refuge for a moment.

'We're okay, love. Thanks to that man, we're going to be fine.'

Maggie nodded and leant her head on her mother's shoulder so she wouldn't see the bright glitter of her tears. Her mother would be fine and that was all that mattered, but she…she knew she wouldn't be fine at all. And it was thanks to that man.

Caleb came back through the house, his footsteps muffled on the carpet, and halted in his stride when he saw through the open kitchen door. Maggie had her head on her mother's shoulder, their arms were around each other. There was something in the scene that was so primal and private that he couldn't intrude. He walked away and waited for a few minutes before coming back, coughing as he did so to make them aware of his presence. He could have sworn he hadn't just seen what he had when Maggie turned around to face him with a bright smile on her face.

'We'd better get going.'

'Fine, dear. I've held you young people up long enough.'

They said their goodbyes and finally left.

As the car pulled out of the drive, Maggie turned to Caleb. 'That day—the day you came to the house—you said you wanted to use it as a bolt-hole… Would you really have moved in?'

Caleb had the grace to look sheepish for a moment. It threw Maggie.

'I never really had any intention of using it. Most likely I would have sold it…I think I wanted to get a rise out of you.'

He shrugged. 'What can I say, Maggie? You bring out the worst in me.'

After that she was tight-lipped and distant. He'd never had any intention of moving in, redecorating. And she'd risen to the bait beautifully.

He cut into her thoughts after a while. 'Maggie…I believe you about your mother.'

'Good.' She just felt weary when he said that. She could feel him flick her a probing glance, could feel it heat her skin. Why did she have to be so *aware* of him?

'What's up?'

She took a deep breath and looked at him. 'Nothing, I'm just a little tired…'

And drained and heart sore…

'There's a ball we're meant to attend tonight, but if—'

'No,' she said quickly. 'I'm absolutely fine. We'll go.'

The rest of the journey was made in silence as Maggie fell asleep and Caleb wrestled with countless disturbing thoughts and feelings. Something just didn't…fit. When he'd walked around the house with her mother, all she'd talked about was her first husband, as if he were the one who had just died…and not Tom Holland. Maybe it was some form of self-protection? But he didn't think so. He'd mentioned Tom Holland once and she'd gone pale and changed the subject immediately. All in all, she seemed far too…happy…for someone who'd just been bereaved and not only that. She was far too happy for someone who'd just been disinherited of millions of pounds.

He shook his head grimly. Felt as if he was in new territory, somewhere he'd never wanted to be. The boundaries were shifting. He took in Maggie's sleeping form and stretched out a hand to tuck some errant hair back behind one delicate ear. She moved slightly against his hand and smiled a tiny smile. Something didn't fit…at all. But did he really want to find out what that was?

When they returned to the apartment that night after the ball Maggie kicked her shoes off just inside the door—her feet were aching. Her nerves were on a knife-edge. All evening Caleb had been watching her, scrutinising her. It was making her nervous. She went into the kitchen to put on the kettle. She sensed Caleb come in and lean against the door frame. Finally she couldn't stand it any more and whirled around. 'What…what is it? You've been staring at me all night.'

His eyes ran up and down her body, leisurely and explicit, and she felt a hot flush invade her skin.

'I don't like it.'

'Yes, Maggie, you do.'

He strolled towards her. She couldn't go anywhere. She was backed against the counter and suddenly remembered that other night in the kitchen when she'd practically ravished him. She went even redder.

'My, what blushes. What could possibly be going through that head of yours?'

He was almost touching her. His hand lifted and cupped her jaw, caressing, moulding, his fingers tracing the line.

He fixated on her mouth for long seconds and Maggie's breathing felt far too loud. Her heart was hammering. Her nerves were screaming.

Just do it…kiss me!

Instead, he seemed to wage some inner struggle and met her eyes. He saw the pulse beating at her temple, under the translucent skin.

'Are you going to tell me what that was all about earlier?'

'What…earlier?' She was genuinely mystified and had trouble concentrating when he was so close.

'Your car, Maggie. The whole song and dance to get your mother off the subject.'

She stiffened. He could sense her distancing herself even though she couldn't physically get away. He had that sensation of her feeling cornered again.

'What do you mean? There was nothing going on.'

'Please. Spare me.'

He brought his arms either side of her body. They brushed against the sides of her breasts. She closed her eyes for a split second. It was so unfair of him to question her like this, when she felt so…weak.

He could see her struggle.

Could see the shutters descend over those lovely eyes, which now flashed a stormy green.

'It was nothing, Caleb. She thinks I have some adolescent attachment to the car, but I outgrew it years ago. Believe me, I hated it, couldn't wait to get rid of it.' She shrugged lightly. 'When she saw the new one…she just wouldn't let it drop. That's all.'

He hadn't made millions from not being able to read people and, right now, he knew Maggie was lying through her teeth. But why? And what did it mean if she was? A door slammed in his head. He did *not* want to go there.

He let his gaze wander down. She looked sexily prim and proper tonight. Her hair had been straightened and pulled back into a low chignon. The high-necked designer gown hugged every curve, hiding far too much and conversely revealing everything. He slipped an arm around her waist and pulled her into him. She melted against him, a tinge of pink along each cheek bone. He told himself he didn't care. Why was he even bothering to question her about it, anyway? All he wanted from her was right here in his arms. She was warm and willing and oh, so ready.

'Fine, Maggie, whatever you say…' and he bent his head and moulded her every curve to his hard length, took her soft lips and kissed her until he felt her legs weaken. Then he led her into the bedroom, opened every button on her dress, kissing each piece of flesh as he did so, by which time she was boneless with want and need. As Caleb came over her, dark and powerful, Maggie had one last coherent thought of thanks that he hadn't felt the need to pursue the matter. And lost herself in him. Again.

Caleb woke early. A misty dawn light illuminated the bedroom. Maggie was tucked into his side, nestled close, one leg thrown over his, disturbingly close to a part of him that was already responding to her proximity. An arm was flung over his belly and her head rested on his chest. Her hair streamed out like a silken caress over his other arm, which held her in this close embrace. He wanted to pull Maggie even closer. Breathe in the scent of her hair, stroke that thigh that hovered so close, have her move her hand down until she could feel for herself what she was doing to him. She felt so good—every soft curve and smooth, silky bit of skin. Her breasts were pressing into his side. He was growing harder. He never wanted to let her go.

What?

He tensed. Wide awake now. Violently awake. Without thinking about what he was doing, he slowly and stealthily managed to extricate himself from her embrace and didn't wake her. His body hummed with arousal. She tossed for a second and he held his breath but then she curled away on the other side and he could hear her breaths deepen again. With her back bared, he could see faint bruises. He had done that? Then something caught his eye—on the back of her thigh, he could see a very pink puckering of the skin, a scar of some kind. It looked as if it had been very angry at some stage, but he guessed it was years old. He wanted to reach out and touch it.

That thought galvanised him into action.

Enough!

He was mooning over his mistress as she lay sleeping. His mistress—that was all she was; he had to remember that.

CHAPTER TEN

'MR CAMERON, you're leaving early…*again*?'

Caleb looked up as he shrugged on his jacket to see Ivy at the door of his office.

'Yes. I presume, as the CEO of the Cameron Corporation, I'm allowed that distinction?' Something in her voice had him sharply on the defensive and he regretted it straight away when he saw an embarrassed flush stain the older woman's cheeks.

'Well…of course, Mr Cameron, I never meant to imply for a second—'

'Ivy, I'm sorry. It's me. I'm just tired, that's all.'

'Of course. This deal with New York is trying all of our patience.'

Yes, it was. And all Caleb wanted to do was go home, walk through that door and see Maggie. Two words had him halt mentally. *Home* and *Maggie*. Since when was that designer apartment home and since when did he long to see Maggie?

Since she'd made it a home…since her toiletries nestled alongside yours…since the smell of home cooking greeted you almost every night…since you've been happy to sit in and watch movies…

He cut off his thoughts with a ruthless effort.

'Do you have everything you need for the flight tomorrow?'

'Yes…' he answered Ivy with relief. He hadn't told Maggie about the trip to New York, which he had to leave for in the morning. And why did that make him feel so damn guilty now? He'd never felt the need to answer to anyone before, tell them his whereabouts.

Just then a younger colleague stopped by the door. He hovered nervously at the threshold. 'Mr Cameron, a few of us are going for a drink around the corner…if you want to join us?'

Caleb picked up his briefcase. 'There's nothing I'd like more.' He was oblivious to the smile that lit up the younger man's face.

Much later, when he let himself in, the apartment was still and quiet. Maggie's light floral fragrance hung on the air and Caleb breathed it in. He'd lasted in the bar for as long as he could, but he'd soon become bored with the youthful conversation, the young men trying to impress him, the women brushing past him suggestively.

He dropped his things, shed his coat and walked to the bedroom, already imagining Maggie curled up, warm and soft and silky. He imagined slipping in behind her, moulding her pliant form to his and waking her, making her body come to life… He walked in the door and the bed…was empty. A crushing feeling resounded in his chest. Where was she?

He retraced his steps and looked in every room. A panicky sensation was rising and he fought to keep it down. Maybe she'd just gone to see a movie again…and he suddenly wished he'd been here—they could have gone together. A snide voice whispered that maybe she was out in a bar, looking for company…

About to pick up the phone, he spotted a light coming from the huge glass doors that led on to the terrace. They'd started using it more and more as the weather got better. Morning coffee, breakfast at the weekend. He'd found it far more relaxing than he would have thought. The idea of such domesticity before would have made him come out in a rash, but somehow with Maggie it didn't feel like that. When he thought about it now, despite having other mistresses in the past, he'd never invited them to live with him. Maggie was the first woman he'd spent so much time with. Which was ironic.

He opened the doors and they made no sound. The cool night breeze swirled around him; the sounds of traffic came up from the streets. Lights twinkled across the city. And there was Maggie. Curled up on a deckchair, in an old comfy tracksuit, a shawl wrapped over her. A mug of something beside her. She'd fallen asleep.

And in a flash Caleb knew exactly what had been bothering him from the start. Maggie had never once dressed like she had that night of the seduction in London. In fact, she displayed an effortless, timeless style and everything she wore complemented her unique colouring and figure exactly. So why had she come to him dressed so cheaply that night? Yet more questions rushed in and he couldn't halt the onslaught. Why didn't she ever want to go clubbing? Which he personally abhorred, but still, usually had to indulge in. Why didn't she call ten times a day just to be reassured that he still desired her? Why, when he offered to take her to the newest, most exclusive restaurant, had she screwed up her nose? And why was she so content just to stay in…and read…or watch TV?

It didn't make sense. But, as these questions begged for his attention, he brutally used the desire rushing through his body to drown them out. He walked over and pressed a light kiss to Maggie's lips. Her eyes opened—dark and greenly mysterious against the black night.

'Caleb…'

'Maggie…'

'Where were you?'

'I had to go out…' And why did he feel like such a heel when he said that?

She just put her arms around his neck and allowed him to lift her against his chest. He carried her into the bedroom, where she buried her hurt and allowed him to undress her. He was back so late. Where had he really been? He'd never say and she'd never ask because he didn't have to tell her. He owed her nothing. She meant nothing to him.

'I have to go to New York for a few days.'

Maggie looked at Caleb reluctantly from over her morning coffee cup in the kitchen. She felt tousled and unkempt in her dressing gown next to his pristinely suited, clean-shaven appearance.

'You're going…alone?' She held her breath.

'Yes.' He was terse. He needed to get away—from here, from her…from too many questions, making his head sore.

She suddenly felt a weight lift off her shoulders; the thought of a few days' respite from the bitter-sweet ache of seeing him, sleeping with him every night, was like an oasis in the desert. Her eyes gleamed with relief and he couldn't fail to notice it.

'You don't have to look so pleased, Maggie.'

She rapidly schooled her features, saying flippantly, 'I'm missing you already.'

'Maybe you should come with me…' he taunted, but he knew she couldn't. This deal was important and she'd be far too much of a distraction. But he'd never tell her that and didn't like the way she tensed at those words. 'Relax, Maggie, you can't.'

He drained his cup and left it in the sink, picked up his coat. Despite the feeling of relief that had invaded her, now as she watched him walk away, about to go out the door, she felt a huge well of loneliness surround her. This was ridiculous. They didn't even get on.

But…they did when they forgot themselves for a moment and had something approximating a normal, easy conversation. At times, they did have a remarkable accord, an easiness in each other's company—something she'd never felt with anyone else. But yet, each time it seemed they might actually get close, one or the other would say something and the past would rear its ugly head. Then bed would conveniently take the need to talk further out of the equation. And she knew she couldn't bear to see him walking away because she knew that one day very soon he'd be doing it for good.

'Caleb.'

He stopped at the door and she walked up and pulled his head down to hers. She pressed her mouth to his and kissed him with desperate fervour. With a groan she felt him drop his case, wrap his arms around her back and pull her up, off her feet and into him. He kissed her back with a raw hunger, almost as though they'd been separated for days already.

Shakily he lowered her back down his body and put her away from him. 'Is that so I don't forget you?'

'You'd better go.'

He stepped out and the door closed. Maggie leaned against it but couldn't hold in the shaking that took hold of her body. She would not cry. She could not cry. She went over to the couch and sat down, hugging her arms around herself.

Just another few weeks, that's all…

She was useless, pathetic. She thought back to when Caleb had come home last night and found her asleep, in a tracksuit. She'd meant to change… She was doing so well at maintaining that all-important front…she hoped. But last night, when he hadn't shown, hadn't called, she'd been so weary. She had felt the fight leaving her. And in a way she hadn't cared. He'd never know the full truth and he didn't seem to mind enough to question her. He hadn't even cared enough to tell her he was going away…

She stood resolutely and vowed to enjoy the few days of freedom. Even as she realised that she *was* already missing him. So much for her facetious mocking words. She may as well have been mocking herself.

For the next few days Maggie painted herself into a frenzy, trying her best to block all thoughts of Caleb. He rang every night but the calls were quick, brusque and she felt as though he was just checking up on her. One night she went to bed in one of his T-shirts, breathing his scent in deeply, ashamed of how badly she missed him.

By the weekend it didn't look as if he was going to make it back. The time stretched ahead of her, yawning, empty. Her feeling of giddy relief at having some time alone had long gone. By the time Monday rolled around, missing him was an ache in her chest. Tuesday came and went. At one stage Maggie thought hysterically that perhaps this was it. She'd get a call from Ivy one day to say that Mr Cameron had shipped everything back to England and could she please vacate the apartment by noon.

The phone rang late on Wednesday night. She nearly dropped it, her heart was beating so fast. Her hands were slippy.

'It's me.'

'Hi.' Why did she have to sound so shy?

'I'll be back tomorrow.' He sounded deathly tired. His voice raw.

'Okay. See you then.'

The phones clicked down. Not another word. No *I miss you* or *Can't wait to see you.* Even so, Maggie couldn't help springing up and wrapping her arms around her body, her blood fizzing with treacherous happiness. He was coming back. He wasn't leaving just yet.

The following morning she answered a knock at the door; it could hardly be Caleb already? Her pulse speeded up anyway and promptly slowed when she saw John, his driver. He looked terrible and his skin was grey. Her concern was immediate and washed away any thoughts of Caleb.

'John…? What is it?'

'I'm sorry to bother you, Maggie. It's my heart…I was on my way to the airport but had to stop… It's a stupid angina thing and I need a doctor…I don't think I can pick Mr Cameron up later.'

Maggie led him into the room and took control. She'd have to collect Caleb from the airport. She'd take John's car—she could hardly turn up to meet him in the Mini! She slid her feet into flip flops.

'We're going straight to the hospital. We'll take your car; you can show me the ropes on the way and I'll pick Caleb up.'

'But…'

'No buts, John; you could have had an accident… You did the right thing coming here.'

He let her lead him downstairs, into the car. At the great age of twenty-seven Maggie had, unbelievably, never driven anything bigger than the Mini and took a few minutes to feel the much bigger car. She squashed the nervous feeling and trepidation, not wanting to give John anything else to worry about. With a bright smile that hid her nerves and sweaty hands, she pulled out into the manic rush hour traffic.

Some time later, after making sure John was stable and

settled into a bed in the hospital, she left. She'd have just enough time to make it to the airport. The car seemed even more daunting now when she got in, not having John by her side to point things out.

Through sheer guts and determination, Maggie managed to navigate it out of the city and on to the main airport road. Finally she managed to loosen her white-knuckle grip on the wheel.

Miraculously she found a parking space, managed not to hit anything and sat there for a few minutes taking deep breaths. She smiled wryly at herself; this was certainly one way to take her mind off Caleb, driving a car worth at least a hundred thousand and three times the size of her own. In the VIP airport arrivals area, John had told her where to wait, as Caleb was due in on a private jet. She stood and waited, her nerves coming back a thousandfold. Would he be surprised? Pleased? Angry?

He was tired. God, he was tired. He'd never felt so tired in all his life. His eyes were gritty behind his lids as he waited for his luggage to be delivered to him. And all he could see was Maggie. He cursed himself again. He could have brought her with him. It wouldn't have made the slightest bit of difference to his concentration levels and might have actually helped them. She'd managed to invade his every waking thought, every sleeping moment. He'd hoped that the trip might prove to him that she was losing her hold on him, on his desire. If anything it was even stronger. One night he'd had to endure a dinner party where he'd been presented with woman after woman, available for his pleasure. They'd been stunning, the crème de la crème of New York society, models, actresses. And they'd done nothing for him. All he'd wanted was… Maggie. And it tore him up inside to admit it.

Finally his luggage arrived and he walked out, looking to

the usual spot for John. And then he saw *her*. The joy that ripped through him nearly threw him off balance. He felt dizzy for a second. Was he conjuring her up? She was looking away; he saw her in profile. Her hair a shock of red against her light green cardigan, wrapped around a short shift dress. Bare legs, flip flops.

And then she turned and looked straight at him with those huge green eyes, ringed with the longest black lashes. He saw her eyes widen; she slightly lifted a hand awkwardly and it dropped slowly.

Why was he looking at her so angrily? She steeled her heart, which had somersaulted on seeing him, and hitched her chin.

He came over, face shuttered. Stern. 'Where's John?'

She blocked the hurt that he'd asked for John first and remembered him guiltily. 'He's in hospital—'

'What?'

She put a hand on his arm. 'He's fine. It's an ongoing angina problem and it flared up. I brought him in and insisted on coming to collect you; he was so worried…' She took her hand away awkwardly.

He rubbed a weary hand over his eyes and Maggie noticed how tired he was.

'Really, he's going to be fine. He just needs to be observed for twenty-four hours.'

'Okay.' He looked at her then, blue eyes pinning her to the spot. A hand reached out and he trailed a finger down one cheek. 'And you?'

She gulped for a breath and just shrugged, nodding. She couldn't even speak. She was useless.

'Thank you for looking after John.'

She shrugged again. 'It's fine. I was hardly going to insist he pick you up or leave him there. The car is parked nearby.'

'You drove his car?'

'Yes, Caleb.' Her dry tone belied the turmoil it had taken to drive there.

When they reached it, she couldn't resist saying cheekily, 'I was going to bring the Mini but was afraid your ego wouldn't fit...'

He smiled a rare smile and felt a burst of pleasure at her irreverence; it was something he never encountered. 'Ha, ha.'

He automatically went to the driver's side and Maggie could see him pass a hand over his eyes. He looked pale with exhaustion.

He gestured for the keys. She shook her head. 'You're not driving; you're half asleep.'

'Maggie—'

She was so firm, she surprised him. 'No way.'

She promptly got into the driver's seat and, short of pulling her back out, Caleb had no choice. Frankly he was too tired to argue. He sat in the passenger seat. He could feel his eyes drift shut; couldn't keep them open. His last waking thoughts were that he'd never ever been met by a woman at the airport before, how much he'd liked it...and that he couldn't remember the last time a woman had driven him. And yet, of all women, Maggie had done these two things. And he knew in his exhausted, vulnerable state, before his mind could jump in and deny it, that he wouldn't have wanted to see anyone else there. The darkness enfolded him.

That night, after dinner, Maggie was preparing for bed. In the bathroom, she took her hair out of the clip and it fell around her shoulders and down her back. She couldn't mistake the light in her eyes. For *him*. Because he was back. A flush stained her cheeks. The silk peignoir felt almost painfully sensuous against her heated skin.

This was so dangerous. She knew it. Like being in a car going a hundred miles an hour, hurtling towards a brick wall with no brakes.

She resolutely turned off the light and went into the bedroom. Her heart turned over when she saw the scene in front of her. Caleb, asleep on the bed, sheets pulled up to his waist, chest bare. A lock of hair had fallen forward and he looked so achingly handsome that Maggie couldn't breathe for a moment.

He sleeps...

As if in a dream, she walked over and sat down beside him on the edge of the bed. He didn't move. She reached out a hand and smoothed his hair back and brought her finger to her lip and kissed it before pressing it lightly against his mouth.

Without opening his eyes, he grabbed her wrist lightly. He pressed a kiss against the pulse fluttering against the delicate inner skin. He opened slumberous eyes and Maggie was trapped. He brought her inexorably forward until she was lying against his chest, her breasts crushed against him. He made a slow, thorough study of her face and then down, to where he could see the voluptuous V of her cleavage.

'Caleb...we don't...you're too tired...'

He shook his head. 'Not too tired for this, ever...'

And with a fluid, graceful movement he rolled her over until she was on her back and he hovered over her. With a hand caressing her face, he bent and met her mouth with his, in a sensual onslaught that washed away any resistance. She was as incapable of stopping him as he seemed to be incapable of wanting to stop.

That hand drifted down and over her silk-covered breast,

teasing the aching peak that jutted out against the material. Maggie groaned hungrily, her hands searching and finding his chest, moving, exploring, down, under the sheet where she came in contact with the heated evidence of his desire.

He pulled up her slip, baring her to his hungry gaze. 'God, Maggie…I've missed you… You're like a fever in my blood.'

An answering cry deep within her had her pull her slip up and off completely and they kissed hungrily, passionately, bodies straining together. With uncustomary clumsiness, Caleb found and rolled on protection. And then, finally, he was home…entering her satin flesh. And she was reaching up to meet him. All tiredness and fatigue gone. A distant memory.

That control that he valued so much was slipping again. His aching hardness sheathed in her warmth made him suck in a rasping breath. He opened his eyes and looked down and sank into green depths. As deep as the ocean. Her cheeks were flushed with arousal; he could feel her body start to tense around him.

He tried to hold on…tried to regain some sense of control and couldn't. Her body tautened and arched against his, her arms wrapped around his back. He could feel her hard nipples pushing against his chest and, giving in to the wild surge building through him, he felt himself being pushed to the brink on the wave of her orgasm and for a moment was poised…about to fall down, into the abyss. But, just before he did, before he crashed, he had the most overwhelming desire to experience this, skin to skin. Without protection. He'd never before felt the lack of that contact with anyone and yet here, now…with *her,* the protective barrier felt… somehow *wrong*.

As the carnal pleasure rippled through him and he felt himself explode, he wanted with a fierce primal desire to be spilling deep into her…to brand her, mark her. Seconds later, when the world had righted itself again, when the realisation hit…of what had just gone through his mind, what it meant, his whole body tensed and stilled over hers. Dear God. He wanted to make her pregnant?

That devastating thought drove him to pull free abruptly from her body and he heard her whimper. Their bodies were still painfully sensitive, his own protesting when he moved away—every cell, every inch of him wanting to pull her close and meld her to him again. His body was still hard but now he had to get away…from her…from himself. Was he just going mad with exhaustion? That was all it was. Feeling sudden wry humour at his crazy ramblings, he pushed himself up from the bed and, without looking back at Maggie, went into the bathroom and stepped into the shower.

Behind him, bereft on the bed, tears stung the back of Maggie's eyes but she would not let them fall. She knew how it was possible to make love and want to cry with a broken heart at the same time. Because she couldn't deny it any longer, couldn't deny the certain knowledge that he had her heart, for ever. Every beat was for him. And it would kill her in the end.

CHAPTER ELEVEN

'MORNING.'

'Morning…' Maggie was sleepily shy. Last night came rushing back. The desolation she'd felt when he'd practically run from the bed after making love. She woke up fast. Erected the barriers.

Caleb was propped on one arm, watching her. He took in all the expressions flitting across her face like clouds passing over a sunny day; he felt something dark pass between them. It was the first time she'd woken in the bed to find him there, watching her like this. Even on weekends, he would invariably go into the office for a few hours in the morning, or else he was out jogging, or just…up.

It made her heart speed up. Despite her best efforts to be cool.

'Don't you have to go to work?'

He quirked a brow. 'Trying to get rid of me?'

She shook her head and her glance jumped down to his bare chest. She could feel the heat starting to invade her blood, could feel her pulse jump. She looked back up and Caleb was smiling. She scowled. Damn him and his arrogance. Damn him and his insufferable coolness.

'As it happens, I do have to go…much as I'm enjoying watching you wake…'

He pressed a kiss to her startled mouth and swung out of bed. She watched him walk away into the bathroom and sighed deeply, pulling the covers up. She'd never get tired of looking at his body. When he emerged a short while later Maggie pretended to be asleep. She felt him come close to the bed and willed him away. In the cold light of morning, if he took her, she'd never be able to hide her feelings.

'Maggie, I know you're awake. I'll be home at seven. We're going out tonight.'

And she felt, rather than heard, him leave the room. She opened her eyes and looked out on a cityscape. They were back to normal. Back to the routine. Functions...balls...and this apartment which was becoming a prison.

Only two more weeks...

The words jumped into her head and she sat up, stunned. Only two more weeks, then...freedom. She couldn't believe it. Where had the time gone? She counted back the weeks and yes, sure enough, Caleb only had another ten to fourteen days here, then he'd be due back in London. He'd even mentioned going back. Had she just shut it out of her head? She sank back down. Her mind couldn't contemplate it right now or what it meant.

That evening, she had just showered and was dressed in a towelling robe when Caleb walked into the bedroom. Her heart lurched crazily. She noticed lines and shadows under his eyes and longed to go over and smooth them, tell him they didn't need to go out. But she couldn't because she didn't have that jurisdiction in his life.

His gaze raked her up and down hungrily; she stood in front of him, a clean scent perfuming the air, her skin still pink from the shower. God, he'd missed her today; his body had ached for her in a way that made him very, very nervous. Yet he couldn't think about that now. It was only the fact that he was running late that had him walk past, shedding clothes.

'We need to be ready to leave in fifteen minutes…'

'I'll be ready,' she answered tightly, stung by his lack of greeting, his brusque voice.

He came out into the hall a short while later, arranging the cuffs of his tuxedo. Maggie stood with her back to him, looking out the window.

She'd arranged her hair so it fell in a coiled rope down her back. The dark grey dress was some kind of jersey material and clung to every curve. It was tantalisingly see-through, giving heady glimpses of a pale curve here, a dark hollow there. She sensed him, tensed and turned around. It dipped in a dark V at the front, between her cleavage. Yet…it lacked…something. Why wouldn't she wear the jewels he gave her?

Despite that first impression she'd given him when she'd cockily asked if she could keep them…he had to make her wear them. She never chose to wear them—it was just another facet to her *act*, no doubt. But, a little voice crowed, *yet another anomaly*… Usually women were begging him for more and more. Bigger, glitzier, gaudier. He ignored the voice.

He strolled forward with indolent grace, making Maggie's breath catch in her throat. She'd seen him in a tux many times by now but somehow, tonight, he was more devastating than ever. Was it because she knew his body intimately? Was it because of the way his gaze drifted up and down her body, stopping, lingering…

He presented her with a long velvet box. Her heart fell. She took it hesitantly, opening it with a stunned gasp she couldn't keep in. It revealed an antique earring and necklace set made entirely out of green diamonds, set in platinum. The faintly yellow-green hue caught the light and dazzled her. She felt herself closing inwards.

She looked up, distant. 'More trinkets for your mistress?'

She was used to this. That was it. She was bored by it. Bizarrely, as much as it pained him, it also comforted him.

He took the necklace out of the box and proceeded to place it around her neck, deftly fastening it. The jewel hung just above the valley of her breasts. He took out the earrings and handed them to her.

'Yes…'

With shaking fingers she took them and put them in her ears. She could feel them sway and move against her neck and hair. He stood back. Cold eyes flicked up and down. She felt a chill.

'Beautiful.'

She felt like a brood mare. She was there purely for his pleasure and if he wanted her dripping in jewels then she would just have to put up with the discomfort. But everytime she'd move and feel them sway against her skin, she'd be reminded that, all too soon, he'd be walking away, out of her life and moving on to the next in line, with whom he'd be saying exactly the same words. Placing jewels around *their* necks in the same dispassionate way…or maybe not so dispassionate. Maybe one of them would break through that austere exterior…find the beating heart of the man, unlock his mysteries. Claim him. Her heart felt like a stone.

'Let's go.'

She followed him out, mute and stung. His revenge was already total. Complete. And he didn't even know it.

This function was similar to every other, in that everyone was beating a steady path to bask in the commanding, phenomenally successful aura of Caleb Cameron. As if by merely being near him some kind of Midas touch would rub off. Maggie was enduring the same unfriendly glances from the Dublin socialites, who wondered how she'd suddenly appeared on their scene. And with the temerity to turn up on *his* arm, not even giving them a fair chance.

She'd hardly ever socialised with Tom or her mother in Dublin. But yet, it was a relatively small city and already she'd caught glimpses of some of Tom's old colleagues, making a shudder of revulsion run through her. One of them in particular, who had been as nasty, if not even worse than her stepfather. She prayed that he hadn't seen her, but it was hard, with everyone's focus on Caleb and him clamping her to his side. She endured the dinner, the small talk, people's curiosity when they found out she came from Dublin herself, yet they were too polite to ask how she'd managed to inveigle her way into Caleb's life.

She could feel him loop a casual arm around the back of her chair, close to his, his hand caressing, toying with her neck. Her breath became ragged. She could feel her body respond and crossed her arms to cover the evidence. He turned to look at her; the sheer weight of his gaze made her turn. Everyone around them, the muted music, chatter of cutlery, raucous laughter, faded. A dense, heavy electric energy hummed between them. He caught her hand and lifted it to his mouth, kissing the delicate underside of her wrist. Maggie's breath stopped. Her eyes flared.

Why had he done that?

He let her hand go and turned back to the person on the other side of him. She was confused and muddled and very much afraid of the seething emotions he was responsible for in her breast.

'And where did you say you were from, dear?'

Maggie turned gratefully into conversation with the old woman on her right.

After dinner the guests were free to mingle and dance in the stunning ballroom. Maggie murmured her excuses and went to look for the bathroom. On her way back, just feet from the door, a voice halted her in her tracks. A definite, hard slap of unease hit her between the shoulder blades.

'Well, well, little Maggie Holland. I thought it was you, but my, haven't you turned into a sexy lady?'

Against her will, she turned slowly to face the man behind the unctuous voice.

'Patrick Deveney.'

The small, squat man had bulging eyes that were looking her up and down with such crawling impunity that it held Maggie immobile. He'd been one of her stepfather's closest friends. And for years he'd slimed around Maggie, but she'd always escaped his advances—just.

He moved closer when someone passed by. She was desperate not to show how scared she was or draw attention. She craned her neck to look for Caleb. She couldn't see him anywhere.

'Looking for your…date?'

'Yes…it's nice to see you again, Mr Deveney, but I really must be—'

Suddenly her arm was grabbed in an intensely brutal grip. She gasped as he pulled her into a nearby corner.

'What do you think you're—?'

He looked her up and down again with obvious lascivious intent. 'I haven't had a chance to offer my condolences,

Maggie, dear. You must be so devastated at the loss of Tom…
We didn't even get a chance to mourn him ourselves. Your
mother had him back here and buried so quickly we couldn't
even pay our respects. That's hardly fair, is it? But now I can
offer them to you personally.'

Maggie stared in disgust, unable to move from the explicit
threat in Deveney's voice. His hand on her arm was stopping
the blood flow; the pain was intense. 'Let me go,' she bit out
through the pain, knowing she'd have an almighty bruise.

'You know, Tom would have come after you if Cameron
hadn't been so quick to take revenge; he knew you blabbed
everything. You and that stupid wife of his. *You* caused his
heart attack; you messed it up for all of us.'

She was transported back in time, her skin going clammy
in remembered fear. She stood stock still, knowing that if she
made a move she'd enrage him further and there would be
more pain. Past and present were tangled; the pain wouldn't
be meant for her, never her, it was always her mother. She only
ever suffered if she got in the way. Yet why was she in pain
now? The mist cleared and Maggie came to.

This was *not* Tom. He was gone. She could handle this
bully. He wasn't going to hurt her. With a swift move she
caught him off guard, extricated herself from his grip and delivered an elbow blow to his fleshy solar plexus. He was
gasping and red-faced, but still far too close.

'I was just wondering where you'd got to.'

Caleb. A wild rush of relief rushed through her, but when
she turned, her heart fell. He was glowering, taking in her
flushed face, close proximity to Deveney and the other man's
obvious breathlessness. And jumped to entirely the wrong
conclusion.

Trying desperately to save face, Deveney slid away, saying

nastily, 'You're welcome to her, Cameron, she always was a little wildcat.'

Caleb's temper ratcheted up a few notches. He grabbed Maggie's arm and she had to stifle her moan of pain as his hand clamped around exactly where Deveney's had been.

'Who is he and how does he know me?'

Without giving her time to speak and in so much pain that she couldn't, Caleb was marching her out and away from the building. The driver who was standing in for John materialised with the car in seconds. They got in. Maggie was still shaken— couldn't believe that Caleb had misread the situation so badly.

'He was a friend of Tom's…and everyone in there knows who you are.' She rubbed her arm distractedly.

He was fighting to keep his mouth shut but wouldn't say anything here in the car. Within minutes they were back at the apartment. The front door closed behind him; Maggie circled slowly to face him. A wary look on her face—a guilty look? He couldn't tell but he was willing to bet it was guilt. What could she possibly see in that creep?

He came in and lounged against a wall, hands deep in his pockets. In the dim light of the room, he looked magnificent. Dark and brooding, the blue glitter of his eyes brilliant against she snowy white shirt and black tuxedo.

'So…do you want to tell me what that was? Already lining up my replacement…going for someone you know? Who works the way you're used to?'

'You're sick. I don't have to listen to this…'

She went to walk from the room, but Caleb took her arm again in exactly the same spot. This time she couldn't disguise her pain.

'What is it?' he asked sharply, taking in the way her face had paled and she looked green. As if she was about to throw up.

'Nothing,' she muttered thickly, but couldn't disguise the tears smarting.

He saw the brightness. 'Maggie what the hell is it?'

'Nothing, Caleb,' she lashed out fiercely. 'If you can't see something that's as plain as the nose on your face, then you don't deserve an explanation.' She pulled free and fled for the bedroom, uncaring of where she went, just wanting sanctuary.

He followed her in. 'What is it? You're angry because I guessed right? How could you, Maggie? That man is odious… Tell me, did you kiss him?' He let out a harsh breath, a jealous red mist descending on his vision, his judgement. 'Of course you did. God! Does he really do it for you? He looks to me to be the type who likes it rough…'

The only thing that halted his tirade was the awful stillness that invaded Maggie's limbs. Her eyes were huge pools of unmistakable hurt, her mouth open in horror. He knew immediately he'd gone too far and stepped closer. She backed away so jerkily that she tripped over the bed and fell backwards. In a second Caleb was there, bending over, picking her up. His hand on her arm was too much; Maggie felt faint with the pain.

'What is it…?' he asked urgently.

'My…arm…you're hurting my arm…'

He let go immediately and sat her down on the bed. 'Maggie, did I hurt you? Show me…'

She shook her head—it was swimming. 'Not you…him…'

He cursed volubly. Very carefully, he pulled the shoulder of the dress down and uttered an oath fit for a sailor when he saw the livid bruise of finger marks that was lurid against her skin. 'Why didn't you tell me…?'

'Well, you didn't give me much opportunity.'

No, he hadn't. Had he really misjudged the situation that badly? All he knew was that he'd taken one look and seen red. He wasn't used to misreading anything. Never mind a woman being mauled by some jerk. And it was this woman. Maggie. He wanted to go straight out and find Deveney and beat him to a pulp.

'What happened, Maggie?'

She avoided the question. 'I need to put some arnica on this or it'll get worse.'

He jumped up. 'I'll get it.'

She directed him to find it in her wash bag and he came back. With infinite tenderness he gently massaged it into her skin. She could feel the tears start again. Couldn't stop them slipping down her cheeks. She was suddenly very tired of being on the receiving end of Caleb's cynical mistrust. Tired of having to maintain a façade. And didn't know if she could go on with the whole charade.

But then…when he caught her face and brought it round to his, and his hands cupped her jaw, his thumbs wiping her tears away, and whispered *sorry* against her mouth, she felt herself melt inside. Yes, she could tell him the truth. Yes, she could tell him exactly what had happened. And if she did…she might not have to face his censure any more. But that would be it—the end. For the one thing he'd despise even more than what he perceived her to be right now, would be the certain knowledge that she'd fallen for him.

And now, when he was being so gentle, so tender, kissing her with such sweet, restrained passion, the tiredness slipped away and all she wanted was to cling on to this…for a little longer.

That night they didn't make love. Caleb just tucked her against him, careful to make her lie on her good arm, and held her within the circle of his embrace. When he acted like this, it made it even harder to maintain a distance. Tomorrow— she'd think about it tomorrow, think about building back up her wall of defence. But for now…for now she'd sink deep into the dream…and she did.

A week later Maggie was painting on the terrace; it was a beautiful summer's day. Her thoughts were on that night, almost a week ago. Since then, she'd caught Caleb looking at her a couple of times with something…some light she couldn't define. And when he'd caught her eye, invariably the shutters would come down. But something had definitely changed between them. There was some kind of stillness. A kind of reverence when they made love…*or maybe it was just her ridiculous imagination.*

She furiously stroked her brush back and forth over the canvas, as if to blot out her wayward thoughts. When she heard the phone ring she went in with relief, glad of the distraction. She picked it up. When she put it down she had a frown on her face.

Caleb wanted to see her in his office. For some reason an icy trickle of foreboding skittered down her back. She changed out of her paint-spattered overalls and into simple trousers and a light V-neck sweater. Her hair swung in a plait down her back.

When she arrived on the top floor of his offices, the unsmiling Ivy had morphed into smiling Ivy. 'Maggie, isn't it? Please come through. Mr Cameron is expecting you.'

Maggie hid her bemusement as she followed the older lady to Caleb's office. She knocked and ushered Maggie through the door.

Caleb was standing at the window, looking out over the city. He turned when she came in and Maggie was struck by how serious he looked.

The door closed behind Ivy. Caleb raked a glance over her. 'What is it?' She laughed a little nervously. 'Caleb, you're scaring me…' She thought of something. 'Is it John; is it his heart again?'

He lifted a hand. 'No…it's not John. He's fine and he said to say thank you again for looking after him so well; he was a lot more frightened than he let on. I've sent him home to London to recuperate.'

She shrugged, a little embarrassed. 'It was nothing.'

He walked around the desk and came close. 'You have paint on your cheek.'

She flushed and lifted a hand to wipe it away. 'I never looked in the mirror.'

She couldn't read the expression on his face.

'Maggie, I've finished my work here. I'm going back to London tomorrow.'

Oh, my God…this is it…he's leaving.

Everything felt woolly and fuzzy, as if it were coming from far away. There was a seat behind Maggie and she sat in it, hoping that it didn't look as if she'd fallen into it, which was what she had done. She tried to maintain an iron grip on her emotions. This was exactly what she wanted. Exactly what she'd been waiting for. She looked up and met Caleb's eyes. They were shadowed. God. Was he looking at her with pity? Did he suspect for one second how much this was killing her?

He couldn't.

She feigned the best look of delayed surprised comprehension that she could. 'Oh! So this is it? You're letting me go…'

His mouth tightened. 'Well, technically, I could insist that you come to London with me; you've got one week to work out the contract.'

Maggie stood, galvanised by shock, the bile rising in her

throat. He saw the way she paled, remembered her reaction on seeing the contract for the first time. 'As far as I recall, the contract stated two months or the duration of your stay in Dublin…so technically, if your stay is up tomorrow, then we're out of contract.'

He looked at her steadily for a long moment. A muscle twitched in his jaw. He couldn't deceive her. 'Actually, I have to confess something. That contract was a bogus document…'

Her mouth opened, her jaw dropped.

'When you reminded me about it in Monte Carlo, I drew something up myself on the computer. It was only to reassure you that I was going to keep my word.'

And he had. Her mother had signed papers already, so the house was legally back in her name. This made something drop out of Maggie's chest.

'So…no one ever looked at it? No one witnessed it?'

He shook his head.

She wasn't sure how to take this, how to react. 'Well… thank you.' She backed away behind the chair. The same chair she'd stood behind that night, when she'd come to beg for the house. 'But then…if there's no contract…then there's nothing to stop me just leaving…walking away.'

'I guess not,' he said heavily.

'You're leaving tomorrow…'

'Yes.'

He looked at her. She was biting her lip. He wanted to go over and take her in his arms, slip his tongue between those soft lips, feel her response as he delved in deep and stroked, enticed…but, for some reason, he couldn't. They'd gone over a line. He was letting her go. So why did it feel as though his heart was being ripped from his chest? Why did it feel as if this woman standing in front of him was the only woman on the planet who he'd ever desire again?

She shrugged her shoulders. 'This is it…'

'Maggie.'

She met his eyes warily.

'You could come to London with me… This doesn't have to end here. Now that your mother has the house…we could go on…you could move in with me…'

She backed away, shaking her head. 'Never,' she said in a thin voice. 'Never. You'll never trust me, Caleb. You'll never respect me. And I won't warm your bed until the next woman comes along. I've paid my dues.'

He stiffened. Damned if he'd let her see what her words were doing to him. He shrugged nonchalantly. 'Whatever you want, Maggie.'

Something lit her eyes, a desperation. 'What I want is to go today. I'm going to go and pack now. When you get back, I'll be gone. I can't stay another night.' Then she said, 'Please, don't make me…'

She wanted to get away from him that badly? He felt a granite block weigh him down in his chest. His face closed, eyes shuttered. His mouth was a grim line.

'If you could be gone by the time I get back, I'd prefer it.'

Maggie walked to the door, her legs having bypassed shaking, had gone straight to wooden shock. She turned back for the last time and faced him.

'I never want to see you again.'

And she went out the door.

Caleb's heart was thumping when he let himself into the apartment. He'd seen the Mini Cooper parked outside… She hadn't gone… Did that mean she'd decided to stay on, as his mistress? But as soon as he walked in the door he knew she was gone. Even though her scent lingered on the air, the place felt flat, devoid of energy.

He saw the car key on the hall table. And a note.

I can't accept the car…or anything else. All the best in your future, Caleb. Maggie.

It fluttered to the floor out of his fingers. Sure enough, when he walked into the bedroom, all the clothes were neatly laid out in bags, labelled up for the relevant shops. And all the jewellery was on the dressing table in each individual box. She hadn't kept one thing.

Why?

Inexplicably, this made him sick. If she'd taken everything, as he'd expected her to, it would have made him feel… somehow justified. But wasn't this typical of her? He sat down heavily on the bed. Every step along the way, she had consistently surprised him by not acting the way he'd thought she would. He got up and went out to the terrace. For the first time in his life, he felt at a loss, didn't know what to do…felt impotent. He wanted Maggie. So badly he could taste it.

As he looked out over the city, felt the ache spreading through his limbs, he knew it. And had to acknowledge it. She'd got so far and so deep under his skin…that he'd fallen for her. He slammed a hand down on the railing. Who was he kidding? He'd fallen for her back in London. And, despite everything she'd done…he was so far in love with her now… that he knew he'd never find a way back.

And she never wanted to see him again. Karma. Revenge.

He left the view and went back in, slamming the door shut behind him so forcefully that the windows shuddered. And the next day, when he got on the plane to go back to London, his face was so grim and stern that no one dared speak to him.

CHAPTER TWELVE

'AND the stock shares went through the roof; they just didn't know how to handle the ramifications...'

Caleb tuned out the conversation. His mind couldn't settle and the heavy weight lodged in his chest was threatening to choke him. All he could see, all he could think about, was Maggie. She was everywhere he looked, but only in his mind's eye. He took in the glittering London crowd that surrounded him. The women were beautiful, stunning, bedecked in jewels. Hair perfectly teased, too thin bodies poured into the latest fashions. And it all seemed so vacuous. Meaningless.

He felt cold when he looked at them and studiously avoided their none too subtle glances from right under the noses of their partners. Several times he'd had to catch himself when he'd turned to his side as if to get Maggie's attention, touch her, have her look up at him with those luminous, wide eyes that said so much and yet held back so much. A sense of panic rose and he couldn't contain it as he imagined never finding out what she'd hidden in those unfathomable depths or never seeing her again. Never waking up beside her, never holding her, talking to her. Seeing her face light up. And yet...how could he have these feelings for someone who had done…what she had, for someone who patently didn't feel the same way?

'…Holland…'

'What?' Caleb said sharply as his focus zoomed in on the man looking at him expectantly. Had he just conjured up her name from his pathetic imaginings?

'Holland. Not wanting to speak ill of the dead or anything, but he was one nasty piece of work; it's only a pity he didn't live to see you in control of everything. That really was some coup, Cameron.'

Caleb smiled tightly; he'd never have wished Holland's ultimate fate on him, no matter what kind of a man he'd been and disliked the inference, but before he could cut in his associate was continuing.

'Now that he's gone and can't keep mouths shut, the truth is out. Did you hear—?'

'Spencer, I've really no interest—'

But the other man took no heed, his drink sloshing over the side of his glass in his obviously inebriated state. '…apparently the man had mistresses in every city and he was a violent bastard—'

Caleb had turned to walk away, but stopped in his tracks.

'…terrorised his poor wife for years. The police were called once but of course it all got hushed up…he greased their palms to keep it quiet. Didn't he have a daughter too? I think they said she was the one who called the cops…never saw her but heard she was a little siren—'

Caleb had the other man up against a wall so fast his drink smashed to the ground.

'What did you say…?'

'Cameron, what the devil is wrong with you?' the other man blustered.

Caleb let him go abruptly and strode out of the room, cutting a swathe through the crowd, who watched in stunned silence.

On the basis of those few words, which rang so true it hurt, Caleb knew that he'd just made the biggest mistake of his life. And he couldn't stop the rising tide of panic that gripped him.

His heart rate was doing triple time.

It couldn't be possible. She could have told me... Why wouldn't she have told me?

The world seemed to tilt crazily as he stood on the steps outside. The past two months ran in his head like a bad horror movie. The signs and clues had been there every step of the way, so obvious...and he had ignored them all. How had he been such a fool? How had he been so blind? Had he really let himself become so cynical and jaded and downright mistrustful that he didn't even recognise a true gem when it was right in front of him?

Like a rock hitting a still, perfect lake and the ripples spreading outwards, everything was so clear in his head now that he felt sick to his stomach. And more terrified than he'd ever felt in his life. *This was it.* And he'd thrown it away. He'd thrown Maggie away. Her words came back into his head with sickening clarity. He could even remember the look on her face. She had wanted nothing more than to get away from him so fast...

I never want to see you again.

Harsh lines transformed his face into a mask of haunted pain as he grabbed his car keys from the valet stepping out and took off as though he had a death wish.

Maggie stood at the edge of the water and watched how the spray came in and rushed back, taking the imprint of her feet with it. They sank a little more. She wished she could sink all the way, her whole body submerged in dark bliss where she wouldn't ever have to think or feel again. She gave herself a mental shake and stepped back out of the oncoming waves.

She looked around. Sheer isolation. A huge beach with acres of empty sand. Bordered by green cliffs on all sides, it was in the furthermost reaches of western Ireland. And it was empty because of a freak summer storm that had blown in for the last two days. The crowds hadn't yet returned but already she could see a figure in the distance, way ahead, near the tiny cottage a family friend had lent her for a few days. Her blessed peace would be gone soon.

She looked back out to the sea and breathed in deeply. She was free. Really free for the first time in her life. So why did she feel as though she were still in prison? It was her heart—her heart was in the prison, not her. And she would just have to learn to live with it. In time…she knew the pain would fade, become less.

She turned and walked back in the direction she'd come, hands in the pockets of a light fleece zipped up against the strong breeze, her jeans rolled up to her knees. There was still just that one figure in the distance, far too far away for Maggie to be able to make out if it were a man or a woman. She emptied her mind and looked down, stopping to pick up shells or stones along the way.

After walking for quite a bit, she could make out that it was a man. A tall man. With dark hair. In a T-shirt and jeans. Even from here, she could see a well-built physique. Her heart twisted painfully. What demon god was sending her a look-alike to test her heart? She drew nearer and nearer—could make out more detail. Thick, dark hair—swept off a high forehead, by the looks of it. Broad shoulders. He was looking out to sea and then he turned around. Maggie stopped. Blood rushed to her head, pounded in her ears, drowning out the crashing waves. It *couldn't* be.

But it was. Every cell in her body told her that it was. Caleb. Just metres away. She shook her head as if to clear the image, but he didn't disappear. He was coming towards her. That struck her into action. She could see the cottage on the bluff just behind him and made a diagonal path away from where he was walking, towards home. She could see from the corner of her eye that he too had changed direction, heading straight for her. She couldn't think. Couldn't feel. One foot in front of the other, until she was behind the door. And safe.

'Maggie.'

She ignored his call, walking faster, desperation making it hard to breathe.

'Maggie.' He was much closer, his long strides effortlessly catching up with hers.

She started a small jog and then felt herself caught and whirled around. She looked up, stunned, into Caleb's face. The shells and stones dropped unnoticed on to the sand.

'Maggie. Please don't run away from me. We have to talk.'

She laughed. 'Talk? Caleb, I told you I never wanted to see you again, and I certainly don't now.' She pulled away and started to walk up the hill. Focus on the house, focus on the house.

'Maggie. Please.' He was close behind her. 'You once came to me to beg me to listen to you for five minutes. That's all I'm asking now. Please.'

She stopped and had to shut her eyes at the memories. Pain lancing through her. This would kill her. But damned if he'd know it. She didn't turn around. 'Five minutes.'

She went into the house through the back door. Not even bothering to hold it open for him.

In the small kitchen she turned around to face him, crossing her arms over her chest. Her heart was beating way too fast for what she had just done. Her hair was windblown, face pink from the wind. And she looked more beautiful than he'd ever seen her. And never more distant.

She was pointedly focusing on a point over his shoulder. 'Well? The clock is ticking.'

'Maggie…I'm sorry…'

She looked at him aghast, her mouth dropping open. 'Sorry? What on earth do you have to be sorry for, Caleb? I got what I wanted; you got what you wanted…'

He smiled but it didn't reach his eyes and she noticed lines around his mouth, smudges of dark colour under his eyes. 'I didn't get you, Maggie, not really. And I still want you.'

She frowned, suddenly feeling a little adrift, wanting to know what he meant but not wanting to ask.

He raked a hand through his hair and looked out to the tumultuous Atlantic for a minute.

'Caleb—'

He looked back, blue eyes vivid. 'I know, I know—the time… God, this is hard.'

Her heart squeezed crazily and she tightened her arms as if to stop it.

'I think I know what happened…that night, eight months ago. Someone said something in London and everything dropped into place…'

Maggie felt a sudden fear. 'Did you go to my mother to find out where I was?'

He nodded.

'Did you say anything to her…?' Her breasts rose and fell in her agitation. 'Did you—?'

Caleb put out a hand, coming a step closer. Maggie moved

away. 'No! No, Maggie…I could have asked her, but I didn't need to. I *know*. I just want to hear it from you.'

'Know what, Caleb? Time is really running out—'

He took a deep breath. 'Eight months ago you seduced me that night against your will, didn't you?'

The room went fuzzy for a second and Maggie could feel her legs wanting to buckle but somehow she managed to stay upright. 'Don't be ridiculous,' she said faintly.

But Caleb had taken in her reaction, the ashen tinge to her skin. It made something joyous erupt in his chest. Even as it was just confirming his worst fears. That she'd never really felt anything for him. Just physical desire.

'Your stepfather saw the attraction between us and made the most of it, didn't he?'

She shook her head numbly.

'He made you flirt with me…made you pretend to show an interest…made you come to the hotel that night dressed like a—'

'Stop!' Her mind worked feverishly. He still didn't know that she hadn't been aware until that day. Her heart was still safe. Her arms dropped to her sides unconsciously. 'How… how do you know this?'

'Just something someone said. I didn't need to hear any more…I knew immediately. I can't believe I didn't see it at the time…but I was blinded.'

She tried to figure out what she could say to keep him happy and send him on his way. Looking at him, having him so close, was quickly becoming unbearable. 'He threatened me with something…too huge for me to fight alone.'

'Your mother?'

She sucked in a breath. 'How do you…?'

'You have a bond that goes beyond anything I've ever seen.

And you're like a mother bear with a cub whenever she's mentioned…plus she's inordinately happy for a recently widowed woman who had been left with nothing.' His voice softened. 'Maggie, I heard…that he was violent… Did he ever—?'

'Never me. Unless I got in the way,' she said bitterly. 'Always her, though. And I could never protect her. Nothing could. Not even the police. He was too powerful.'

A vivid image came into his head, a sick feeling. 'That scar…on your thigh…'

Maggie went paler. 'I got in the way one day…when he was…when I tried to…he knocked me out of the way and I fell into the ironing board, the iron…'

Rage filled him. He opened his mouth but Maggie had had enough. She held up a hand. 'Please, Caleb. You know now. Thank you for giving us back the house and for paying off the tax debts… My mother told me. You didn't have to do that—'

His hand slashed the air. 'Of course I did. It was my fault your mother was put in that situation; it was the least I could do.'

Maggie continued; she wanted him gone. 'I'm sorry I deceived you too eight months ago, but it's over. Please, just go.'

For a second he half turned as if he was going to go. Maggie held her breath, a hollow feeling spreading throughout her body, but then, abruptly, he came back. She was rooted to the spot.

'No…Maggie, I won't go. Because I want to know—once Holland had died and there was no threat any more, why didn't you try to defend yourself?'

'Would you have believed me?'

'Perhaps not at first,' he conceded. 'But it wouldn't have taken much to convince me. I'm not such an ogre and I would never have taken the house if I'd known.'

'I know…' she said quietly.

'So…why?'

Her brain had become mush. *Why, indeed?*

When he said it like that now, so simply, she could have cursed herself. It had simply never occurred to her. Her main priority had been self-protection, but hadn't she ironically gone the most self-destructive route? Since she'd seen him again…her brain had become so scrambled that she'd happily sabotaged herself. In an effort to block out reality and to have him on any terms. His terms. She was pathetic.

'Because I thought you wouldn't believe me…' It sounded weak to her ears.

'So you allowed me to use you, take you as my mistress, let me make love to you almost every night…put on the not very successful pretence of someone who was the complete opposite to what you really are?'

'But it was…' she breathed, not realising that she was giving herself away spectacularly.

He felt triumphant. He lifted a brow. 'Then why leave everything behind? The clothes, the jewels, the *car*?'

'Because they weren't mine,' she answered simply.

'Exactly.' He looked smug. 'Any other woman would have cleaned out the lot. And more. Believe me.'

She felt as though she was being wrung out on a rack; he was stretching her and stretching her to breaking-point. Her voice came out brittle and harsh. 'Look, Caleb; what do you want? I can't tell you any more…'

But he was relentless. 'I bet you made it all up, just to keep up the front… College? You put yourself through it and never took a penny from Holland, am I right? Probably lived in a bedsit with mice rather than take his money. Lovers? I know you weren't a virgin, but you weren't far off it, Maggie.'

She went even more ashen at his uncannily accurate assessment. He noted it with something close to fury rising in his chest—fury at himself.

He was immovable, implacable. She knew instantly the only thing that would move him would be the one thing that would kill her. But if it meant she'd get rid of him then she had no choice. Before he guessed the full truth, if she could protect herself from at least that…

She squared her shoulders. 'It was cockroaches, actually, and you want the truth?' She tossed her head. 'Here it is. The truth is that I had one lover before I met you, in college. And I didn't know what Tom had planned until…until…' She couldn't do it.

A stillness entered Caleb's body. He came closer and Maggie could feel the heat from his body reach out to caress her, touch her. He had to go…*now*. She had to be strong.

'That day.'

'The day of the date?' he queried sharply. Too sharply.

Maggie turned away in agitation, arms around her body. 'Yes, damn you, yes!' She turned around again. 'There! Are you happy now? I didn't know until that day, so in case it's not completely obvious, let me spell it out for you. I had a crush on you, Caleb, a monumental crush. I believed that you possibly felt something for me too and I *stupidly* believed that you *wanted* to take me on that date, to get to know me.'

'Maggie…'

She could see a flare of something in his eyes. Her voice shook. 'Don't you *dare* pity me, Caleb Cameron. I don't need your pity. It was a crush, that's all. Desire. Tom followed me to Oxford Street that day and made me buy that…that dress…' a shudder of revulsion went through her '…then he told me what he'd do to my mother if I didn't comply. I had no choice.' The fight went out of her; she looked away. 'But then…I just…'

'Couldn't go through with it.'

She looked back quickly and a shiver of something inde-finable ran through her. He was looking at her with…not pity…something else and it made her silly heart speed up. He came close, too close, and only then she became aware of the fat tear sliding down her cheek. She didn't even know she'd been crying. He reached out a hand and she jerked away.

'You've been minding her for a long time. And you came back to Dublin to escape, didn't you?'

Why did he have to say that so gently, as though he really cared? She nodded slowly, more tears slipping hotly down. His hand came out again. This time she couldn't move as he wiped his thumb back and forth. The contact was too much. A broken sob escaped and, with a curse, Caleb closed the distance, pulled her forward and into his arms. He held her for a long time. Until the sobbing had stopped. Rubbing her back as though she were ten years old.

But then she didn't feel ten any more. She felt like a grown woman whose body was springing into life, pressed as she was, tight against the length of him.

She tried to pull back but he wouldn't let her go.

'Caleb…let me go, I'm okay now…'

She was sure she looked awful; as a freckled redhead, she didn't do pretty crying.

'I can't let you go.'

She looked up. 'What?'

She felt rather than saw him shrug. His eyes bored down into hers. 'I can't let you go. I'm afraid that if I do…I'll wake up and have dreamt all this and that I'll never see you again.'

A taut, pregnant stillness seemed to surround them.

'But…you can go now. Leave. You don't want to see me again.'

'No. *You* don't want to see *me*.'

Maggie's brow creased as she took in a vulnerable light in the depths of Caleb's eyes. It couldn't be. She shook her head. 'Caleb, stop confusing me. Let me go.' She tried to pull away again, a little desperately. There was no give.

'Just tell me one thing, Maggie… Was it really just a crush?'

She felt him stop breathing. Nodded her head slowly. And inexplicably, started to drown in his eyes. She just…couldn't do it. Couldn't lie. Feeling the last vestiges of her defence and fight fall away, leaving her limp and defeated, she stopped nodding and slowly shook her head.

A surge of mounting hope moved through him. 'So…if it wasn't just a crush…was it something more?'

She was feeling boneless. All that existed were those mesmerising eyes. She nodded again, barely aware of what she was saying yes to, only aware that she wanted Caleb to keep holding her. For ever.

Caleb tried to contain himself but could feel the tremor building all the way upwards from his feet. 'For the past two months…and now…is it still there?'

She broke out of the seductive trance. She could feel the tears well again. 'Please Caleb…don't tease…don't make me say it.'

He lifted his hands and framed her face and she could feel them trembling. 'You don't have to…I will. Maggie Holland, I love you. I love you so much that if you can't tell me you love me too then I'm going to walk straight into the Atlantic and never come back because my life would not be worth living.'

A hard shell seemed to crack open around her. She clung on to his eyes, searching, seeking…and could see nothing but pure love shining back. Could she trust?

She had to trust.

With a very shaky voice she said huskily, 'That'd be an awful waste because I love you too…I've loved you since the moment I set eyes on you.'

'Oh, Maggie…' He groaned and lowered his lips to hers, taking her mouth in a sweet kiss, hunger barely checked, but there. He stopped and pulled back. 'When I saw you that first time…I fell so hard and then when I overheard Holland talking about using you…I cynically assumed you were in on it too. It was easier to see you as an accomplice than face up to my true feelings…I'm so, so sorry; when you tried to stop and tell me—'

Maggie just shook her head, putting a finger to his lips. 'It *was* pretty damning and we'd only just met. You had no idea who I was…'

She wound her arms tightly around his neck and, stretching up, pressed her mouth to his and urged him to kiss her deeper, harder. They pulled apart after a few seconds, breathing harshly. She touched his face wonderingly.

'Are you here? Is this real?'

He laughed shakily. 'I hope so because I'm about to get down on one knee and propose.'

'Caleb…' She watched, open-mouthed, as he knelt down before her. Tears blurred her vision again. They just wouldn't stop.

He took her hand. 'Margaret Holland. Will you please become my wife? So that I can spend my life loving you, minding you, protecting you…'

'But…but you never stay in one place for long…your work…'

His voice was raw and husky, pulling at her heart. 'Maggie, I'm so tired. I'm tired of living under the shadow of my parents' disastrous marriage. I'm tired of working so hard. It's time I delegated. I want to settle down, have babies…with you. Wherever you are, or want to be…this house…we could buy this, live here, *anywhere*, just as long as I'm with you. I never believed this could happen to me, but…' he shrugged with endearing vulnerability '…you're my home…and I want to come home, so much.'

She shook her head, her lip wobbling, tears still streaming, and got down on her knees to meet him. 'Oh, Caleb…you're my home too. I love you so much it scares me…'

They looked at each other for an intense moment and he cradled her head before kissing her again. Her eyes were closed and she was breathless when he pulled away finally, both blissfully unaware of the hard floor under their knees. Then Caleb stood and pulled her with him. 'I have something for you.'

She was incapable of speech, touching her lips, feeling them tingle from the kiss, wanting to pinch herself to see if she was really awake. She wiped at her cheeks as he led her out to the front door and there, parked in front of the house, was her battered Mini. Exactly as it always had been.

She clapped a shocked hand to her mouth. Wide-eyed, she looked at Caleb, shaking her head. 'But…how…I mean, it was a tin can…'

He grimaced. 'Just seconds away from it. I started tracking it down after that day your mother spilled the beans, even though you professed not to care, somehow, I knew.'

'But that was…weeks ago.'

He shrugged. 'I was fighting a losing battle even then, trying to keep you in the little box I'd built around you, but more and more I was beginning to suspect things weren't as they seemed, but it was still easier to mistrust you than look at my real feelings…'

She looked away reluctantly from the intense emotion blazing from his eyes.

'Is that how you came down here? That's at least five hours…in a car that doesn't go over forty miles an hour…'

He rolled his shoulders. 'Don't I know it and it was more like eight hours.'

He brought her round to the back of the car. 'This was Plan *B* in case you weren't going to listen to me.'

There at the back of the car were tin cans tied on pieces of string hanging off the bumper, trailing on the ground, and a huge sign, which read:

I love you, Maggie. Please marry me?

'Believe me,' he said dryly, 'it's the only thing that convinced your mother to tell me where you were.'

The laughter bubbled up out of her and she gripped his hand. He brought her round in front of him and she could feel the slight tremor still evident in his hands as they smoothed back her hair. The awe on his face, as if he couldn't really believe he'd found her. It made her heart soar and flip over.

She wrapped her arms tightly around his waist. 'The answer is yes, yes, yes…'

She gave him a shyly coy look. 'About those knots in your shoulders…'

He relaxed visibly and Maggie exulted in the gift he was giving her, that she was giving him. After so much heartache. Perhaps now, she could finally be safe…and happy.

He bent low to whisper in her ear with husky promise, 'We have so much to talk about, catch up on…but first let's see about making those babies…'

With one graceful movement, he lifted his most treasured possession and carried her over the threshold of the tiny cottage that clung to the edge of a beautiful beach, with the waves pounding just metres away, and into their new lives.

Chosen by him for business,
taken by him for pleasure…
A classic collection of office romances from
Harlequin Presents, by your favorite authors.

Coming in September:

THE BRAZILIAN BOSS'S INNOCENT MISTRESS
by Sarah Morgan

Innocent Grace Thacker has ten minutes to persuade
ruthless Brazilian Rafael Cordeiro to help her.
Ten minutes to decide whether to leave and lose—
or settle her debts in his bed!

Also from this miniseries, coming in October:

THE BOSS'S WIFE FOR A WEEK
by Anne McAllister

www.eHarlequin.com

HPI2664

REQUEST YOUR FREE BOOKS!

2 FREE NOVELS PLUS 2 FREE GIFTS!

PASSION
GUARANTEED
SEDUCTION

THE ROYAL HOUSE OF NIROLI

Always passionate, always proud.

**The richest royal family in the world—
a family united by blood and passion,
torn apart by deceit and desire.**

By royal decree, Harlequin Presents is delighted to bring
you The Royal House of Niroli. Step into the glamorous,
enticing world of the Nirolian Royal Family. As the king
ails he must find an heir. Each month an exciting new
installment follows the epic search for the true Nirolian
king. Eight heirs, eight romances, eight fantastic stories!

Coming in September:

BOUGHT BY THE BILLIONAIRE PRINCE

by Carol Marinelli

Luca Fierezza is ruthless, a rogue and a rebel....
Megan Donavan's stunned when she's thrown into
jail and her unlikely rescuer is her new boss, Luca!
But now she's also entirely at his mercy...in his bed!

**Be sure not to miss any of the passion!
Coming in October:**

THE TYCOON'S PRINCESS BRIDE

by Natasha Oakley

www.eHarlequin.com

HP12659

Mediterranean N I G H T S™

Experience glamour, elegance, mystery and revenge aboard the high seas....

Coming in September 2007...

BREAKING ALL THE RULES

by

Marisa Carroll

Aboard the cruise ship *Alexandra's Dream* for some R & R, sports journalist Lola Sandler is surprised to spot pro-golfer Eric Lashman. Years after walking away from the pro circuit with no explanation to the public, Eric now finds himself teaching aboard a cruise ship.

Lola smells a career-making exposé... but their developing relationship may force her to make a difficult choice.

HM38963

HARLEQUIN *Presents*

BILLIONAIRES' BRIDES

Pregnant by their princes...

Take three incredibly wealthy European princes
and match them with three beautiful, spirited women.
Add large helpings of intense emotion and passionate
attraction. Result: three unexpected pregnancies—and
three possible princesses—if those princes have their way....

Coming in September:

THE GREEK PRINCE'S CHOSEN WIFE
by Sandra Marton

Ivy Madison is pregnant with Prince Damian's baby—
as a surrogate mother! Now Damian won't let Ivy go—after
all, he didn't have the pleasure of taking her to bed before....

Available in August:

THE ITALIAN PRINCE'S
PREGNANT BRIDE

Coming in October:

THE SPANISH
PRINCE'S VIRGIN BRIDE